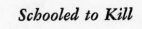

Schooled to Kill

Dell Shannon

Schooled
to Kill

William Morrow and Company, Inc.

New York

Make little weeping for the dead,
for he is at rest; but the life of
the fool is worse than death.

—Ecclesiasticus 22:11

Chapter One

THE DOG was asleep when it happened. Asleep on the pile of coats and sweaters in the back seat of the topless convertible ambling along the freeway. The crash woke him, and then he was thrown violently out of the car, his erstwhile bedding along with him, and landed still on top of the coats on the shoulder of the road.

He was stunned momentarily, shaken and bruised but not really hurt. There were loud noises, loud voices, screams. By the time the dog got to his feet, shaking and frightened, all the cars had stopped moving out there, and people were crowding around the center of the road. The dog whimpered and tried to join the crowd, searching for his own people; but a man shoved him away with angry words; and then a loud screaming thing was coming nearer and nearer, and the dog panicked and ran. He ran, lumbering, along the shoulder of the road, a long time past the lines of stalled cars, until he found a way off that road and was on a narrower street where there were houses.

Then he was lost. He wasn't a dog to stay panicky for very long, but he felt very lost. He'd never been in a city before, and it bewildered him. He went on walking, sometimes trotting along, investigating yards and the few empty lots, but nothing was familiar. . . . By daylight he had found his way to a long straight street lined with buildings, and presently there began to be people in the streets, which pleased him, for he didn't know he was a dog at all; but most of them steered a wide course around him or just ignored him. He was alone and lost, and he felt very sorry for himself.

He didn't like the noise and confusion of the street, and turned back up a narrower street where smaller buildings stood. He was sitting on the curb there, forlorn, when a car slid up to the curb and stopped and a woman got out. She spoke to him in a friendly tone. "Hello there," she said, and held out her hand and patted him. "What are you doing here?"

The dog, extremely pleased, smiled widely at her and offered his paw politely. She shook it and laughed, but then she went on and walked around the corner out of sight. The dog's ears drooped despondently. There was, however, the car. The front window was down, and with some difficulty he heaved himself up, almost stuck halfway through, panted and struggled and flopped down clumsily into the seat.

He approved of the car. It had the right smells. It smelled of children and also of cats. The dog was very fond of both children and cats.

Something had happened to change the world; and his people had gone away. It was an empty feeling inside him; but he was of a philosophic disposition, and largely took life as he found it. Here at least was temporary haven. Until his people came back.

He curled up on the floor of the back seat and went to sleep.

Landers was alone in the Homicide office when the new one came in. It was one-thirty of a Monday afternoon in February, just a week since the Lieutenant had come back to work, and they were being kept busy. Even a little more so than usual.

That wanted rapist-killer on the Ten Most Wanted list, Patrick Albert Rooney, hadn't been picked up yet. He might be the X they wanted here for the rape murders of the Moreno girl and Juliet Romano. There were flyers out; they knew he'd been here, at least, ten days ago; he might still be here, or he might not.

They hadn't any leads at all on the murder of Mrs. García.

It was the first week in February, and as usual in Southern California, at some time early in the year, it had turned strangely mild. They'd get more cold weather and rain before April, but right now it was sunny and warm.

And Landers was alone in the office because half an hour before, with Mendoza, Hackett, and Higgins just back from lunch, they had had a call—the body of the Pickens child found at last, up in Elysian Park. Nobody had really expected her to be found alive, the eight-year-old reported missing four days ago. So now it was Homicide's business, and one like that they wanted to get after fast—pick up anything and everything they could in the way of leads—so the three of them, Sergeant Lake said, had taken off in a hurry, picking up John Palliser on the way as he came in, and Lake had dispatched a mobile lab truck to meet them.

The kids, thought Landers, coming back from lunch to hear that. It was the innocent kids that got you. The little eight-year-old kid, dead. They hadn't had a child rapist in a while; that was probably what it was. At first they'd thought they had one on the Moreno girl, who'd only been twelve, but the next one that boy had killed had been nineteen, and the Moreno girl had looked a lot older than she was, well developed, so they were thinking now he was just a rape killer period. Could be this Rooney; he'd used a knife before, and a knife had been used on Rita Moreno and Juliet Romano.

Landers was typing up a report on the latest body from Skid Row, yet another stupid idiot with an overdose of heroin in him. He was alone in the office; it was Piggott's day off and Glasser and Grace were both out on something. Landers was feeling grim about the little Pickens girl, and wondering what they were finding up there, when Sergeant Lake rang him. "So what now?" said Landers.

"Well, something I think you'll want to hear about," said Lake. "A funny something. You'd better listen to this guy."

Resignedly Landers got up and went out to the anteroom. Standing beside Lake's desk was a beefy-shouldered, nervous-looking young man in tan work-clothes, who was saying, "Honest, I never even fired off a gun. In my life. They wouldn't take me in the Army accounta I'm deaf in one ear. I got water in it swimming once."

"Yes, yes," said Lake. "This is Detective Landers. You tell the tale to him."

"A detective," said the young man. "That's good. I never been in trouble with the law, I never even got a traffic ticket. The whole thing's just crazy, that's all. But I thought I better come tell you guys about it, and I don't know all your different departments or whatever, place this size, I told the guy downstairs, in the lobby or whatever, I said it was about a murder and he sent me up here."

"You've got some information about a murder, sir?" asked Landers.

"That's right, only it ain't happened yet, see. The murder. I oughta said, my name's Loveluck."

"*Lovechuck?*" said Landers.

"No, no. Luck. Loveluck. It's a funny name, ain't it? But people remember it because it is funny. Gabriel Loveluck, that's me." He was about twenty-five, and he wasn't overly tall but stocky and strongly built. He had large light-blue eyes and a nose that turned up slightly and big square hands.

"Well, what have you got to tell us, Mr. Loveluck? Come in here and sit down, won't you?" Landers took him into the sergeants' office, gave him a chair, and sat down at his desk.

"Thanks. You're a *detective?* I mean, you don't look very old," said Loveluck dubiously.

"I'm a detective," said Landers equably. It wasn't his fault that he had one of those faces that would go on looking about twenty until he was a grandfather. "What have you got to tell us?"

"Well, it's just crazy," said Loveluck. "I guess you won't hardly believe it. Neither did I at first. But, swear on the gospel, it's so. I was in this place for lunch, see—an hour ago, maybe hour and a half. It's a place over on Fourth, Papa Joe's place."

"That's its name?"

"No, no, its *name* is the Roman Villa, but it's just Papa Joe's place—nothing fancy, not very big, but serves good eats and it ain't expensive. See, I work at the Shell station along up from there—toward San Pedro—and it's handy. I'm just sittin' there havin' another cup of coffee when this guy comes up to me. He says, would I like to make a thousand bucks, and I said sure, but what's the catch. He says, come on outside, I tell you, nobody twistin' your arm but you look like a guy maybe might be willin'. To *me* he says that! I ask you, do I look like a murderer?" asked Loveluck indignantly.

"What?"

"Yeah, yeah, I never heard such a crazy thing. Offered me a thousand bucks to *kill* somebody! I thought it was a gag— I went out and sat in his car with him, no harm hear what he had to say—and he says he'll give me a thousand bucks to kill this dame. A woman yet. Crazy. He says he's out on bail, he's coming up for trial in a couple weeks for armed robbery and this woman's the only witness against him and he don't want to go to jail. Crazy."

"I will be damned," said Landers. "Do you know him? Had you seen him anywhere before?"

"Never laid eyes on him before today," said Loveluck promptly. "Or, so far as I know, did he ever see me before. Which makes it all the crazier. He said his name was Bill Bessinger and the woman's a Mrs. Naomi Spears. Well, mister, I was so flabbergasted I didn't know what to say, if you get me— Me! I never even had a traffic ticket, I'm an honest man, I go to church regular—Baptist—and maybe I'm not so smart as some people, I never graduated from high school, went to learn a trade instead—but right while I'm trying to get my mouth to shut—he thinks *I* look like a guy'd do a thing like that!—I think, gee, the cops oughta know about this, and if I turn him right down like my first instinck is to do, naturally, he'll maybe go on the run and they can't find him. So I pretend like maybe I'd be interested, and say Maybe, and I'd like to think about it, and all. So he gives me a paper with his name and phone number on it and goes off, and I hightail it right here to you guys, and come to think I shoulda called the boss and told him where I was. It's crazy."

It was fairly crazy, but that kind of thing was not new to any experienced cop. "I will be damned," said Landers, and picked up the phone. "Jimmy, get me Goldberg's office. . . . Landers, Homicide. Have you got a record on a Bill Bessinger who's due to come up for trial pretty soon?"

"Oh, my, yes," said the voice of Sergeant Betts. "Why? Well, the count is armed robbery, his third time round in California, so just maybe the judge will hand him a real sentence for a change. Witnesses? Yes, the woman he held up—a Mrs. Naomi Spears. Owns a little general market over on North Main. She was alone in the place when he came in with a gun. What's Homicide's interest? He hasn't killed anybody—yet."

"You'll be hearing," said Landers. "I just wanted to check, thanks." He put the phone down.

"The more I think about it the madder I get," said Loveluck. "He thought *I* look like a guy who'd kill a dame for a thousand bucks! I should sue him for libel. I never missed a Sunday at church. I don't even smoke. I never so much as touched a gun. I—"

"Yes, well, we're interested to know about this anyway," said Landers. "You'd better make a statement, Mr. Loveluck, and we'll see how the Lieutenant wants to play it."

"How to *play* it? I s'pose you know where this guy's living—if he's on bail. Go and arrest him, I should— Offering me, anybody, a thousand bucks to—"

Alison came briskly out of the beauty salon, walked down to the corner, and turned up to where she'd luckily found a slot for the Facel-Vega on the street. She had a date for lunch with Angel Hackett, but would go home first to change into the new suit. She slipped into the driver's seat, glanced in the rear-view mirror, then started the engine and headed up toward Yucca, went around the block back to Hollywood Boulevard, and down to Laurel Canyon, and up that broad winding boulevard to Rayo Grande Avenue.

Thank goodness, she thought, that Máiri was back so good with the twins, so reliable. With due care for cats—the twins were more visible—she turned into the drive and pulled up. As she got out of the car backward, reaching for the coat she'd decided she didn't need after all, her eyes fell on the back seat and widened.

"For heaven's *sake!* What are *you* doing here?"

The dog smiled at her and got up, climbed clumsily over the seat and flopped out into the drive. He was a large shaggy dog with absolutely no tail. He had a big round head and big feet. Most of his body was a deep blue-gray, but his head, chest, and all four feet were white—rather dirty white now.

"And where in the name of guidness did *that* come from?" said Mrs. MacTaggart, coming round from the back with some cut roses in one hand.

"For heaven's *sake!*" said Alison crossly. "The stupid thing was on the curb where I parked, it must belong around there somewhere—why it got in the car, heaven knows, but I'll have to—"

"'Tis an English sheepdog," said Mrs. MacTaggart interestedly. "Nice dogs they are."

"It looks part bear," said Alison. "Of all the annoying things! It's after eleven now. And I'd better put it on a leash of some— Has it got a collar? Maybe there's an address—"

"Very friendly the beastie is, at least."

The dog swiped at Alison's cheek with a long pink tongue as she bent over him. In the depths of the shaggy coat she found a chain-link collar and a small tag attached. The dog squirmed and pawed playfully. "Be quiet, I can't read it if— *Well!*" said Alison.

"Is there an address, *achara?*"

"There is not. It just says Cedric. Which I suppose is your name," she said to the dog.

The dog balanced himself on his round, tailless end and offered a polite paw. They both laughed, and Alison said resignedly, "Oh, well! I'll just call Angel and say I'll be late. But of all the nuisances— Come on, Cedric!"

Up in Elysian Park, beyond the tamed landscaping around the Police Academy building, Mendoza stood with Hackett and Higgins and Palliser looking at the small body over which Dr. Bainbridge was bent. With anger and pity they looked, but impassive expressions, and the interns from the waiting ambulance smoked and tried to look impassive too. The squad-car men who'd answered the first call, from one of the Parks and Recreation employees who had found the body, looked angry and muttered at each other.

"We knew she was dead," said Mendoza. He dropped his cigarette and stepped on it. "The only answer, a rapist. Eight years old." Marla Pickens, a thin blonde youngster small for her age, by the description. Missing from where?—they couldn't even be sure of that. She'd gone to school last Thursday morning, but she'd forgotten a book needed for her first class and the teacher had given her permission to go home for it. Six blocks from the public school on Logan Street, over to Laguna Avenue where she lived. But Mrs. Margaret Pickens worked at the Broadway from nine to four, and she hadn't been home, so nobody could say whether Marla had got home and then started back to school, or had been picked up on her way home. Men from Missing Persons and Juvenile had been out, the Homicide men could guess, along all the way Marla would have taken to go home, asking if anyone had seen her—seen anyone approach her. Nothing apparently had showed—though now that it was Homicide's business, they'd want to talk with those men.

"It's the kids get you," said Higgins suddenly, savagely. "The senseless bloody things we see. The grown-up idiots, they've brought it on themselves. Some way. But the kids—" he balled one big fist.

None of them added anything to that. It was, of course, all too true. And Higgins was probably thinking of Stevie Dwyer and that hit-and-run last November. Not that *that* had been entirely bad luck: it had stirred Higgins up finally to propose to Mary Dwyer, and even now, nearly four months later, he seemed a little surprised that she'd actually married him. And Stevie was going to be all right eventually.

Which Marla Pickens wouldn't be.

Bainbridge hoisted his tubby self to his feet and said, sounding less irascible than usual, "She was probably raped. I'll give you details when I've done an autopsy, but I'll bet on that. Call it ninety-six hours, give or take."

"As we might expect," said Mendoza, "that morning—on her way home or back to school." He lit another cigarette.

"After four days it's the best I can do. Stomach contents may pin it down some."

"All right, doctor," said Hackett. "We know. And so we go break the news to that poor woman, and go cover all the ground that's been covered, and turn up damn all. If anybody'd seen her, they'd have said so by now. A hell of a thing to work. Do you think it ties in with Moreno and Romano, Luis?"

Mendoza shook his head. He looked dapper and elegant, as usual, in the silver-gray herringbone, Homburg in his hand. He also looked coldly savage. Mendoza now had some hostages to fortune himself. "I do not. We decided that boy is after the grown-ups—he made a little mistake with the Moreno girl, who looked at least eighteen. Besides, there wasn't a knife used here. Can you give us a provisional cause, Bainbridge?"

The doctor shrugged. "I'll have a guess she was strangled. By accident or intention, take your choice. But it could have been something else—you can see she's been beaten."

"Yes, doctor."

The lab men had been prowling around. This area up above the Academy had been left largely wild, and there were no paths: clumps of young trees, many lower bushes and wild grass. Now Duke came up from a growth of young birches down a little slope, with a plastic bag held before him.

"Tells you a little something, anyway," he said laconically, exhibiting his find. It was the book. The schoolbook. A thin but good-sized book, looking a little shabby, with a bright-green cover and the title *Learning Together*.

"Where?" asked Mendoza.

"In there. At the foot of a tree. Just as if it'd been dropped."

"Um." Mendoza's long nose twitched. "*¿Cómo no?* I wonder. Show me where." He followed Duke, and the other men came after them. "So, did he bring her right up here—nice quiet spot—after he'd got her? And just maybe had she been knocked out, and came to and began struggling again about here, and dropped the—I'm woolgathering."

"How'd she hang onto the book if she was knocked out?" objected Hackett.

"Yes. And why did she hang onto the book at all? This far?"

"There's nothing here," said Duke. "There was just the book there, by the tree." There wasn't anything. No footprints—the grass wouldn't take those—no blood, no scuffle marks, nothing.

"But," said Mendoza, rocking a little back and forth, heel to toe, "just down that slope is the nearest road. For a car. Elysian Park Drive. I wonder."

"That sergeant from Juvenile," said Palliser thoughtfully, "said the mother's a nice woman. Respectable woman. Said the little girl'd been warned about talking to strangers and so on. And that area—where she'd have been—is crowded. People around. How did he get hold of her?"

"So she'd been warned. She was only eight," said Higgins heavily. And he really couldn't help thinking of Laura, who was only not quite ten. Who had also been warned. And yet as good a girl as Laura was, she was young and kids forgot, not meaning to. Not having the experience or judgment.

"Well, we have to work it," said Hackett. And, of course, nobody with youngsters of his own at home could look at it as just another job.

"Was it done right where she was found?" said Mendoza abruptly. He turned and led the way back there, up the little slope. It was a smallish clearing, natural, surrounded by high-growing shrubs. Bainbridge hadn't moved the body much; it had been pushed half under one of the bushes. Delicately, Mendoza stepped nearer; they all looked. The small pathetic body, blackened and bruised, had dark dried blood on it here and there—and most of the clothes described by the mother were there: the light-blue cotton dress, with red trimming and buttons, the red corduroy jacket bundled half under the body. She was still wearing the white bobby socks and black strapped shoes, but the red hair-ribbon was missing. As were the cotton panties and cotton half-slip. The dress had been half torn off the body.

There were marks on the grass, where possibly a little struggle had taken place: probably not much of a struggle, this place or another—an eight-year-old small for her age.

Bainbridge said slowly, "Maybe. Maybe, Luis. Let the lab get what they can off the clothes and so on. There's enough blood around. If it wasn't here it happened, she was brought here right away, still bleeding."

"I think," said Mendoza, "I'd like to talk to the fellow who found her. What's his name? Josiah Kane. Yes indeed."

"*Now* what's in your mind?" asked Hackett. "You don't think—?"

"Who knows? Not many people," said Mendoza, "come wandering up into Elysian Park. This far past the Dodger Stadium. It's not like Echo Park or MacArthur. And who might think of Elysian Park, as a nice quiet handy spot to accomplish a rape, but somebody who has occasion to be up here at least now and then? I don't say yes or no—I'd just like to talk to him. And anybody else who works for Parks and Recreation and comes up here on occasion."

"And I think," said Higgins, "a better bet is Records."

"Oh, it could be. *Tal vez*. But we'll be looking everywhere. I just say, let's be thorough." Mendoza clapped his hat on and stepped on his cigarette.

"And pray he doesn't get the urge again before we drop on him," said Higgins, watching the interns lift the little body onto a stretcher.

"You are such an optimist, George," said Mendoza.

"Let's say more of a realist."

"So I'll go break the news, and you can go back to base and start looking in Records." And that, all of them were aware, was typical of Mendoza: so easy to delegate the unpleasant duty, and he wouldn't enjoy it, but it was his job to do. "And you know," he added dreamily, "I've got a little feeling—just a little feeling at the back of my mind—that this wasn't, maybe, altogether the random thing. At all."

They stared at him. "What d'you mean? Random? What

else? One like that, the nut, the pervert, seeing the kid walking down the street—" Hackett suddenly added, "Yes, and we might get something asking other kids around there if anyone's tried to coax them—"

"Yes, it looks like that," said Mendoza, "doesn't it? Come on, let's get on it."

"You don't mean to tell me," said Jason Grace incredulously, "that this Bessinger just walked up to an utter stranger and offered him a grand to do a murder?"

"That's just what, apparently," said Landers. "Can they come much more stupid, I ask you? Loveluck—my God, what a name—And I can just hear what the Lieutenant'll say. Crazy, my good Lord. But we'll have to do something about it, I suppose. After all, murder is murder. Before *or* after the fact."

"Never laid eyes on the creature," said the householder. The last householder on this block: Alison had covered both sides of the street, it was twelve-forty-five, and she was starving. The dog wasn't: Mrs. MacTaggart had fed the dog generously before Alison embarked on her search.

"What? But he was right there, across the street, when I first saw him. He got into my car—He must belong somewhere around here—"

"Never saw it anywhere around here, sorry." The door closed with finality.

"Well, honestly!" said Alison. She looked down at the dog. "What am I going to do with you?"

Cedric felt a little anxious at the annoyance in her voice. He lowered his shaggy forequarters in an attitude of prayer and sneezed violently. The long hair over his face flew back momentarily and revealed a wall-eye on the left side, horribly wild and staring. She burst into laughter. "But you've got to belong somewhere! For heaven's sake, I suppose I'll have to take you along—I'm late enough already—have to advertise, or—"

He offered her a placating paw. "You're a con man in disguise," said Alison.

Chapter Two

"I GUESS I knew from the first she wasn't coming back," said Margaret Pickens mournfully. "That she was killed. Like that. Some fiend." She sobbed dryly. "I tried to do my best, see all the kids were taken care of, but—You didn't mind that I called Rhoda?" When Mendoza had broken the news to her she'd asked if she could call Rhoda before she'd started crying. "Because she's my best friend, and she'll be as heartbroken over it as me. So good to the children—"

Mrs. Pickens was a little woman already defeated by life. She'd always expect the worst, thought Mendoza, while going through the motions to ward it off. She was about thirty-five, with lifeless light-brown hair, and a thin sallow face with a long nose, and she was too thin. She was very neatly and cleanly dressed, and she looked dowdy. Laguna Avenue, one of the old streets in the Echo Park area, was drab middle-class: old single houses, larger old houses made into apartments, and shabby old four-family flats. This was one of those, a five-room apartment long in need of new paint, a general face-lifting.

Mrs. Pickens' husband had walked out on her four years ago, and hadn't been heard from since. She lived on her salary from The Broadway, didn't hold with taking charity, but it was hard sometimes, she said, the children needing things. Eileen, the seven-year-old, was at school: Henry, the four-year-old, played with a stuffed horse across the room.

"But I don't understand how anybody could've picked Marla up, like they say. I'd always warned her careful about strangers, especially men, and she wouldn't't've got into a car or anything like that. Around here some sections aren't too good, you know, I always warned her and Eileen particular. And somebody would've seen, I should think—city streets—"

Cover the streets again, he thought. Where other men had asked questions before. Coming home from the school on Logan Street, Marla would have walked down Logan to Sunset Boulevard, down that to Echo Park Boulevard, and some four more blocks to Laguna. Two of those streets were fairly main drags. Yes, and, of course, in crowded situations people weren't noticing: concentrated on themselves.

"Marla never said anything to you about a strange man approaching her, or—?" And that would have been asked before too.

"No. No, she never. And she would have. I told the other policeman. She was a good girl. No trouble. She always did what you told her. A *good* girl." Her weak blue eyes filled with tears. "And she knew how worried I was for money—almost the last thing I remember her saying to me, that morning she left for school, she said, 'Mama, I'm going to grow up real fast so I can get a job and help you earn for the rent and all.' I never had a minute's worry about Marla—a good girl—"

The door to the hall opened and another woman came in, a fat, pretty, dark young woman about Mrs. Pickens' age. "Oh, Margaret, I come just as soon as—oh, you poor dear! I been so scared it'd turn out like this, tried to cheer you up, but I knew in my bones—oh, that poor darling girl!"

"Oh, *Rhoda!*" sobbed Mrs. Pickens. The other woman sat down beside her on the couch, one arm around her, and sobbed companionably.

"But I mustn't, because it's no *use*," said Mrs. Pickens, sitting up with effort. "It won't do Marla any good now. And I've got the others to think about. Only I can't understand how it happened." She mopped her eyes. "You knew her, Rhoda.

Such a good obedient girl. And quiet, but she had plenty of sense. She wouldn't've let—"

"I've wondered about it, dear. I know. But she was such a little thing, a good strong man—one of these *fiends*—could've just pulled her into a car—"

Mrs. Pickens sniffed and put her handkerchief away. "I guess that's so." She turned a dull stare on Mendoza. "Oh, I guess I ought to say, you didn't meet Mrs. Foster before, sir. I guess there's different policemen on it now. What'd you say your—?"

"Lieutenant Mendoza." There was a cheap glass ashtray on the table beside the sagging old chair, and he was smoking quietly, giving her time. "Mrs. Foster."

The fat young woman turned an open, interested gaze on him, giving her eyes a final wipe. And it wasn't pretended emotion; but, he judged shrewdly, any emotion with her would be ephemeral—shallow. A kind, easily moved, sentimental, and probably rather stupid woman, he thought. Kind, yes; it was in her big dark eyes. She had an unbelievable complexion, peaches and cream, and curly dark hair. But her body billowed in too-rich curves under a too-gay Hawaiian print shift, and her plump bare little feet were thrust into run-over old moccasins.

"The police have been awful good," she said. "I certainly do hope you catch whatever awful fiend did it."

"So do we, Mrs. Foster. You knew Marla too? Did—?"

"Oh, I don't know what I'd have done without Rhoda. The baby was only a little thing when Henry left me, I couldn't have—but Rhoda was so good—"

"Now, I liked doing it, honey, don't you fret."

"You see, working and all, but I couldn't leave the children alone, so young, but Rhoda looked after them—it's just the baby now, the other two in school, but what I'd have done without her—Not as if we were real old friends, either, I haven't got any old friends out here, we just got to know each other in the park and at the market, like. So good—"

"Oh, now, I like doing it," protested the other woman, a little embarrassed, a little innocently flattered. "Never had any of our own, both of us crazy about kids, and I pick up a little extra baby-sitting like that," she told Mendoza. "Not that I'd charge Margaret—and Frank makes enough to get by on fine, we do all right. But when I think of that poor innocent child —a good girl, like Margaret says—why, she was a big help looking after the baby, a real responsible little girl. Regular as clockwork, she 'n' Eileen turning up after school, our place a kind of second home for them, you know—And some *fiend*—"

"Just a minute," said Mendoza softly. "You say that she'd usually come to your home after school instead of here?"

"Mostly she would, and Eileen too, of course. They were used to being with me, and Margaret don't get home until nearly five. Then they'd—"

"And where do you live, Mrs. Foster?"

"Why, just over on Morton. Six, eight blocks."

Morton Avenue. The exact opposite direction from the school. "Did you tell any of the other police officers that, Mrs. Pickens?"

"What?" She looked bewildered.

"That the two girls usually went to the Fosters' as a—mmh —second home, after school?"

"Why, I don't guess, exactly like that—I said I had this good friend look after the other children while I was out looking for Marla—Oh, I was wild! When Eileen told how she was let to come home after her book, and never came back—and the principal said he called the apartment, but of course nobody was here then—and it was after dark and—"

"Yes. A Lieutenant Carey—did you tell him that the children usually went to the Fosters' after school?"

"I don't remember," she said vaguely. "I don't think he asked me about that. I was wild—"

Mendoza regarded the pair of them with concealed exasperation. Two good, decent, respectable females without the average amount of common sense between them. Just how far had they delayed the hunt? "Mrs. Foster," he said rather sharply. "Was Marla at your home the day before? On Wednesday afternoon, after school?"

"Why, yes, she was. I said she and Eileen most generally come to our place when school lets out, and then they went on home when Margaret'd be there. What? Well, I don't recall exactly, but I guess they left about the usual time—four-thirty or a quarter to five. To go home. Here."

"Yes," said Mendoza. "Do you remember if she had that schoolbook with her?"

"Oh, I couldn't say. I don't know as I ever laid eyes on it. I guess she must have had it, the papers said the teacher told—"

"A big green book. *Learning Together.*"

"I couldn't say."

"You don't remember if she left it at your place? Or took it home when she left?"

Rhoda Foster looked vague. "I couldn't say, honestly. I wasn't paying any attention. I didn't notice any such book around, but it could've been, I suppose."

Mendoza brushed his neat mustache the wrong way and then carefully smoothed it back again. He couldn't blame Carey of Missing Persons or whoever had come out from Juvenile for missing this: neither woman had had the sense to mention it. "Mrs. Pickens. Did Marla have a key to the apartment—this apartment?"

"Why, no, of course not. She was only eight, I wouldn't—"

"Then if she was coming back here after her book, how would she have expected to get in? The door was locked, I suppose?"

"Well, I don't know. That is, I mean, sure the door was locked. The other officer asked that too. I guess she could have been meaning to ask Mrs. Calvin to let her in—the manageress downstairs. I don't know . . . I guess I knew from the first it'd be something awful like this. Marla dead."

"It's God's will, and you just got to be brave, Margaret. Anything we can do for you—you know Frank'll be all broke up too—never any of our own—"

"Mrs. Foster," said Mendoza. She looked at him a little impatiently. "Were you home last Thursday morning?"

"Why? Why, no, I wasn't. Not till about noon. It was a nice sunny morning, and I took the baby—Henry there—down to Echo Park. He likes the swans, and I had some knitting—

What? Well, I guess I left about eight-thirty, early anyway. Just after Margaret left him off like usual."

¡Mil rayos! thought Mendoza. These stupid females, the very relevant evidence withheld with not the remotest intention. The men working this up till now not knowing that the good friend who looked after the Pickens children wasn't doing it just that afternoon while Mrs. Pickens looked for Marla: that it was the regular thing.

So, when Marla left school to get her book last Thursday morning, she might just as well have been heading for the Fosters' as her own home: might have forgotten the book there instead of at home. And heading for the Fosters' on Morton Avenue, she'd have been going the opposite direction from the school. Look up a map, see exactly where.

He suppressed annoyance. "Did you lock your apartment when you went out, Mrs. Foster? Then? Thursday morning?"

"A house, we've got a house," she said. "Well, I locked the front door, but that side door's got warped or something and won't lock. I been after Frank—What? Oh, sure, Marla knew that. What you *mean* exactly? I thought—"

Females! thought Mendoza. He didn't feel like wasting time explaining. He got up.

"These females," said Jason Grace. He rolled report sheets in triplicate into his typewriter. "She must have been mighty surprised." His regular-featured chocolate-brown face looked amused, cynical, a little sad. "One of those you'll-be-sorry-when-I'm-gone kind. She'd done it before—taken the very careful overdose just before the husband got home—her knowing when he'd get home—so he could call the doctor in time. Only this time he'd got mad enough at her that he went and tied one on instead of coming home. Little surprise for Nelly to find herself facing St. Peter. *Or,* more likely—" He started to type.

"Yes, very funny," said Palliser inattentively. He was reading Mr. Gabriel Loveluck's statement. "We ought to do something about this, Tom. What a hell of a funny thing."

"Isn't it. I want the Lieutenant to say what. With all the

rules and regulations these days, it might be smart to get something besides just that statement."

"I suppose," agreed Palliser, and Hackett and Higgins came in. "What have you got?"

"A lot of potential legwork, what else?" said Hackett. He and Higgins had been ferreting around the sex files in Records. "And reasons for argument. There's no shortcuts on the routine."

"Did I say there was?" asked Higgins reasonably. "All I said was, records can go just so far. It may be a first job. He may have a pedigree some place else. What we've got here is a month's hard work, and I just wish to hell there *was* a shortcut."

The sex files, from a place like L.A., were extensive and varied. They had been through them last month, too, on the Moreno and Romano murders; now they were looking for something different, the rapist who liked little girls; and, of course, the one they wanted might not be there at all, as Higgins said. But it was a place to start.

They started to look at the pedigrees Hackett had pulled from Records, the suggestive ones. There were forty-six men in the first bunch: men who had attempted to or had actually molested children. Go and look for, and at, them. Question them. Hope the X they wanted was among them. And if he wasn't, or if they couldn't prove it—

Mendoza came in with two men behind him. He was looking annoyed. He said, glancing at the sheets in Hackett's hand, "Hold everything. We've got something new. We won't be hunting up the punks with pedigrees for a while, but going house to house. I think. You all know Lieutenant Carey. Sergeant Conway, Juvenile. Come into my office."

"What's turned up?" They followed him in.

"She might not have been heading for home at all." He told them about Rhoda Foster and the Pickens children's second home. Carey and Conway, who had just heard about it, merely looked disgusted. "All we want from you," said Mendoza to them, "is—you did all the looking up to today—whatever you got on that aspect. Did you turn up anybody at all who saw the girl on her way from the school to Laguna Avenue?"

"No," said Carey.

"No," said Conway.

"It made me think," said Carey, "that maybe the kid had decided to play hookey. Once she was away from school. Because you'd think somebody would have noticed her. Well, all right, on the main drags people are busy. But there are a couple of gas stations along Sunset there, a car-wash place, people in a position to be noticing the street. And she'd have been going along residential streets too. Say between about eight-fifteen and eight-forty-five. Housewives dusting their front rooms—or out gardening—you'd have thought somebody would have seen her. I wondered. Now we hear this. So maybe we were asking in the wrong places. And four days ago—five, really—who'll remember?"

"As against that," said Mendoza, "there is the fact that the average muddleheaded citizen is concerned about kids. Interested in this—sympathetic. But the sooner we get on it the better. I want everybody out." There would, of course, be householders away from home, the necessary repeat calls. Talking to the citizens could be time-consuming; you had to give them time to ransack memories leisurely, hope they were sure. "On the map, you can see it. She'd have gone down Logan to Scott, probably, down to Echo Park Avenue, and then down to Morton. Call it five blocks. And mostly residential. A lot of people to ask."

"A little job," agreed Grace seriously; he'd abandoned his report to follow them in. "We'd best get on it. And pray we catch this one fast."

Glasser poked his sandy head in the door. "Extra special confab? That Progress Place thing was nothing. Type up a report, *finis*. Progress Place, my good God. Over the other side of the yards, ramshackle little old hen coops, the riffraff and flotsam. Two old fellows living together, retired S.P. laborers. The Fire Department says, for pretty sure accidental. They had an old oil stove to cook on, and they were both winos. Probably both tighter than ticks, and tipped over the stove—wonder it hadn't happened before. A lot of stupid people around. In fact, what we see mostly. What's going on?"

Mendoza explained economically, and Glasser sobered. "The little Pickens girl. Also a lot of evil, as Piggott would say. So, we'd better get on it. A couple of hours left of the working day." It was three-fifty.

"Are we punching time clocks on this one?" demanded Higgins roughly, and passed a hand over his craggy features. "Sorry, Henry, but one like this—"

"Well, I guess not, at that," said Glasser. "I guess not."

Sergeant Lake looked in. "We just had an anonymous call. Very shy gent. Says that Patrick Rooney is now in a bar over on Main, the Aztec Grill."

"Oh, for God's sake!" said Hackett. "Rooney, when we've got—"

"Like women's work, never done," said Mendoza sardonically. "J. Edgar does want him, Arturo. Also for rape. You and George go look—he's big and mean, and if he is there we don't want to lose him. You can join us later, whether or no."

"Oh, *this* guy!" said the bartender at the Aztec Grill. He looked as if he'd just crossed the border, swarthy, mustached, dark liquid eyes and a flashing white grin, and he spoke pure Brooklynese. "Why didden you show me the picture, instead o' all that so many feet and pounds like. This guy. All the tattoos. Yeah, he's been in here. Was just in here a while ago. Oh, boy, Feds want him, hah? There's a reward maybe? I'll watch for him again. Naw, I never noticed which way he went, he goes out. Maybe half an hour ago he left. He can put it down all right. Had four double Scotches, straight, in about half an hour. Well, I'll keep an eye out for him and let you know. What's he done?"

"Murder," said Hackett.

The bartender didn't bat an eye. "I'll watch for him. Shame you missed him this time."

So Hackett and Higgins went on up to Scott Avenue and joined the rest of them asking the questions. Last Thursday morning, did you happen to see—?

Mendoza turned into the drive of the house on Rayo Grande Avenue at six-forty. He was going back to do some more leg-work down there after dinner, so he didn't slide the Ferrari into the garage, but stopped on the apron outside. As he got out, a dog barked sharply very near by, and he jumped.

The spotlights in the backyard were on, and at the foot of the back steps Alison was bending over a dog. A dog tied with a length of rope to the railing of the steps.

"*¡Qué diablo!*" said Mendoza. "And just where in the name of God did *that* come from?"

"Oh, darling, I didn't hear you—This is Cedric," said Alison. "He—"

"Cedric. And just what is Cedric doing in my backyard? Who—?"

"Oh, for goodness sake," said Alison, "don't jump down my throat, Luis. I couldn't *help* it. I've done nothing all day but run around in circles with this idiotic dog, but he is rather a darling and we've got to find out where he belongs. He—"

"He does not belong here," said Mendoza. "The cats—"

"—jumped into my car. And all the tag on his collar says is *Cedric*. And I went to every house on that block—and then I was meeting Angel and she fell in love with him and said we must—whoever owns him will be fearfully worried—so after lunch we went to every single building along that block, and nobody had ever seen him before, or knew anything about him. So I said—"

The dog balanced himself on his round tailless rump and offered Mendoza a paw. "The cats—"

"Now be nice and shake hands, Luis. He's trying to be polite, you might—Well, the funny thing is, about the cats," said Alison, "he seems to *like* them. I couldn't take him to the pound, after all—"

"Why not?" asked Mendoza, reluctantly accepting a large shaggy paw. The dog swiped his tongue across Mendoza's mustache. "*¡Ca!* A sycophantic appeaser, like all dogs."

"Luis!" said Alison reproachfully. "The pound! I *wouldn't*. He belongs somewhere. But I couldn't bring him here unless

I knew he was all right—no mange or anything—I thought we could advertise—so I took him to Dr. Stocking—"

"*Naturalmente.* Wasting good money—"

"And he went all over him and said he's fine. He said he's a purebred Old English sheepdog and can't be more than a year old, if that. And he must belong to somebody, Luis, and he's a darling. A clown. And when I brought him back, Bast was asleep on the back step, and he went right over and kissed her nose, waggling all over—he seems to like cats—Of course Bast was furious, and swelled up and hissed at him and ran, and he looked so *aggrieved,* it was funny. He—"

"Is no concern of ours," said Mendoza firmly. "I'm not so crazy about dogs. Especially large shaggy dogs. Cedric, *Dios.*"

"I've put an ad in the *Citizen,*" said Alison. "Please, Luis. The *pound*—sometimes they don't keep them more than two or three days. We *couldn't*—"

"Well, I do not approve so much of the damn hygienic pound either," said Mendoza grudgingly. "If you keep the thing tied up—"

Cedric bowed his forequarters in a prayerful attitude and put one paw over his face. Alison laughed, and he jumped up and smiled at her widely.

"And the twins went mad over him. You can imagine. He's wonderful with them—he likes children too. He's such a darling, Luis, and somebody must be terribly worried—the ad'll turn up his owner, surely—"

"You keep the thing tied up," said Mendoza. "All right. But I won't have the cats upset. A monster like that."

"He *likes* them. He must be used to cats. And children."

"Well—"

Cedric edged up and licked Mendoza's hand. "A cadger," said Mendoza. "Knows which side his bread is buttered on. Like all dogs. Subservient."

"He's just being friendly, for heaven's sake. Just likes people. And he must belong somewhere," said Alison.

"So, find out where and get rid of him," said Mendoza.

Cedric lay down and put both paws over his face.

"Well, I said I'd put an ad in the paper. The least we can do. A purebred dog, he must—"

"An idiot," said Mendoza. "Getting lost. Cats never get lost. Cats—"

Higgins got home at nine o'clock. He and Hackett and Palliser and Grace and Glasser and Mendoza had put in the overtime down there on the streets where Marla Pickens would have been last Thursday morning—maybe. But that, they knew now. They'd turned up pay dirt almost at once, a Mrs. Goulding, who was a childless widow with arthritis, and who lived in a ground-floor apartment on Scott Avenue. She'd told Grace, yes, she'd been sitting at her living-room window, as on most mornings, she got up early and she liked to watch the children pass on their way to school, the sweet young things. And a while after they'd all gone by, still sitting there, she'd seen a little girl walk back down the street alone—perhaps eight-thirty it had been—all alone, yes, and she thought a blue dress and red coat. She had wondered about it then. After school had opened.

So now they knew, for pretty sure, that Marla had passed that way. Late on it, and they hadn't turned up another blessed thing. From anybody. Yet.

"Have you had anything to eat?" asked Mary. Her gray eyes smiled at him. He didn't believe it yet, that she was his wife. That he had a family—a real family.

Stevie (the doctors said the brace could come off in a couple of months; still therapy needed but he'd be O.K.) smiling at him, "Hey, George, I finished *Ivanhoe* today, it was real great, I sure liked it." Stevie reading more these days, which pleased Mary.

And Laura, not quite ten, "Can you listen to my new piece now, George? I want to—Miss Jeanie said I'm doing real well—"

"Really well," said Mary, smiling.

"*Really* well. George—"

He wasn't usually demonstrative with the kids, Bert Dwyer's good kids—but he bent and hugged Laura hard a minute.

"I'd like to hear it, Laurie." And Laura too, like all the nice little girls, warned about not talking to strangers and all the rest, but the polite, nice little girls raised to be friendly and trusting and helpful (did you want to raise them *not* to be?) and so terribly, vulnerably unaware of all the evil and perversion and ill-will—You could only pray, keep her safe. You could only—

"I picked up a sandwich," he said.

"I'll warm over the stew," said Mary. Her gray eyes were soft on him. For once he wasn't looking at her. He was worrying about Laura. All you could do—

Chapter Three

FIVE minutes after Mendoza came into his office on Tuesday morning Hackett looked in and said, "How's the lost pup? Angel was telling me about it."

"*¡Por Dios!* I will not have that monster annoying the cats. Alison's put an ad in about it. I suppose it must belong to somebody."

"It could have got loose from a car, people just passing through. Angel knew a woman came by a Great Dane that way, she—"

"Dogs!" said Mendoza. "Supposed to be the great brains. Getting lost. Cats never—"

Sergeant Lake looked in and said those men from the Parks and Recreation Department were here. "So we'll see that Kane first," said Mendoza, lighting a cigarette. The men from Parks and Recreation had been politely asked to show up this morning; Mendoza and Hackett would talk to them. Everybody else except Palliser was wandering down on Marla's route, asking questions. It was Palliser's day off, and doubtless his Roberta would be dragging him through more houses for sale.

But if Mendoza thought he'd had a hunch about the men from Parks and Recreation, it was a dud. Josiah Kane, who had found the body, was about sixty, a tough, withered, old New Englander who grudged his words. He looked indestructible,

and very stiffly upright, and after talking to him for five minutes both Mendoza and Hackett mentally wrote him off as a
possible rapist. Mr. Kane was mighty sorry about the little
girl, grown-ups getting killed was bad enough, but little
girls, well, things at a pretty pass nowadays. "And these young
fellers we get. Tchah. No idee about an honest day's work.
Work for the city, you get security, that's the idee. Don't
matter about doin' an honest job. Tchah. That's why I was
up there yestiddy. That plantin' of young birches, four-year-
olds. See how they was comin' on—I put 'em in myself, last
year. There ain't much to do up in Elysian, we don't keep it
all trimmed and tidied up like a reg'lar city park—just the
part round the Academy buildin'. I hadn't been up there in
a couple weeks, nor I don't think nobody else had either. No
work scheduled up there. I just went up on my own, have a
look at them birches. Pretty trees, birches are."

They talked to the four other men who would have occasion to be up in Elysian Park, if rarely, and they all looked
absolutely normal and ordinary. All married, all sounding
open and sincere.

"N.G.," said Hackett when the last of them went out. "I
thought so when you had the brainwave."

"Mmh, yes. It was just a thought."

"So I'll give you one." Hackett leaned his bulk back and lit
a cigarette. "Anybody might think of Elysian Park. Right off
the bat. The nice quiet spot for rape, once the victim was
snatched and, presumably, in a car."

"¿Cómo no?"

"Sure. There it is, sticking up like a sore thumb from any
place within miles, down here. The big green hill right in the
middle of town. So, we say he snatched her off the street—
the nut just happening to spot the kid alone—and maybe very
easy, Luis, the little girl small for her age, she mightn't have
had time to yell—and he's got her in the car, maybe knocked
out, but anywhere around there, Scott Avenue, Echo Park
Boulevard, it's a crowded residential area, he won't take the
chance of doing it there. Inspiration, nearest and handiest
lonely spot, Elysian Park. Entrance not eight blocks off."

"Sí. It could be that way I just keep thinking about that book," said Mendoza, shutting his eyes.

"Why?"

"Well, if you reason it out, Art—how come she still had the book up there? If all that's so? How had she hung onto it? Snatched off the street—and in that crowded area nobody noticing? Wouldn't she more likely have dropped the book the second he grabbed her?"

"I don't know," said Hackett slowly. "Instincts are funny. Could be—she'd just gone back to get it, you know—she'd have hung onto it instinctively. Oh, by God, I just saw that—so we know at least she was on her way back to school because she *had* the book—"

"So quick on the uptake. *Sí.* And we know she'd left the book at the Fosters'. And furthermore," said Mendoza, "Morton Avenue is more of a main drag than the streets she'd have been on otherwise, and more traffic there as a rule—all the more likely that by chance the nut would be there to notice— The book. I just wondered."

"I don't see there's much to that," said Hackett, and the inside phone rang.

It was Scarne from the lab. "Some prints on that book," he said, "but they're all the kid's. Sorry."

"Oh," said Mendoza. "What about the clothes?"

"We can't do everything at once. Tests going on now. We'll let you know."

"Thanks so much," said Mendoza.

Landers came in. "You said to report back about now. What on? We've got another sighting down there—another woman, nearer the school, noticed her. Starting out."

"Mmh," said Mendoza. "Well, this Loveluck, Tom. My God, what a thing. Talk about silly. But I'd just like to get a little more solid evidence on Bessinger than Loveluck's statement, for the grand jury. It would amount to a charge of conspiracy to murder, after all." He regarded Landers sardonically. "You really don't look much like a cop, and I suppose you've got some old work-clothes around."

"Now what's in your mind?"

"Hunt up Mr. Gabriel Loveluck—that Shell station—and tell him to call Bessinger and arrange a meeting—tonight if possible. You go along, and have Gabriel introduce you as a pal who's going to help him with the job. You'll have to play it by ear—Bessinger may be suspicious, but considering what we know about him he may not. You will, of course, have the little microphone hidden in your breast pocket."

"Fun and games," said Landers. "What a thing. All right, I see. I'll go talk to Gabriel."

"And I suppose," said Hackett as Landers went out, "with the P. and R. employees duds, we'd better do some work elsewhere."

"Oh, dear," said Mrs. Rose. "Oh, dear. I did wonder if that was the little girl I saw. That morning. Do you think it was?"

"We don't know, ma'am," said Piggott. "This was about a quarter of nine?"

"Oh, well, I think so. I was out in the front yard. The roses. My husband hadn't got round to cutting them back last month —There are quite a few children pass along here on the way to school, but earlier, you know—I don't *know* any of them—but this was later, nearly an hour later, and it just crossed my mind—I remembered it the next day when it was in the news about the little girl missing—"

"Yes, ma'am," said Glasser patiently. "Do you remember anything about what she looked like? Her clothes? You thought she was seven or eight?"

"Oh, around there. I don't remember about her clothes, or —Just a child walking past. Do you think it *was?* That one? Such awful things happen these days—"

They thanked her and went on out to the street. "So you had a little brainstorm, Matt," said Glasser. "We'd figured, after we'd placed her along Scott coming away from the school, she'd have gone back the same way."

Piggott's thin dark face took on a look even gloomier than usual. Piggott tended to be a pessimist. "It just occurred to me, Henry. When I looked at that school. It does sit a bit nearer—the front entrance—to Montana Street than Scott. She

might have gone that way round. So now we can say probably she did. If we find somebody else along here who saw
her."

Morton Avenue, two blocks up from where they stood, took
a little jog and became, suddenly, Echo Park Boulevard. Along
here the street was not yet parallel to Echo Park and the lake,
but converging on it. At the end of this block, the other way,
Montana Street crossed, and a block and a half down Montana
was the elementary school Marla had attended.

"So we go on asking," said Glasser. They moved on to the
next place. This was the kind of territory where the house-to-
house routine was long and tiring; there were few single houses.
The street was lined with old courts and apartments, which
meant that they had that many more individuals to find
and talk to. But it was the routine that often broke cases, so
they plodded on. It was getting on for eleven o'clock, and
they'd been at this since eight-thirty.

At the three old apartments before the big house on the
corner, they questioned thirteen people found at home. They
got, for fairly sure, all there was to be got at those places, for
it turned out that none of the tenants with front windows had
jobs: housewives, old people on pensions. Nobody had noticed
a little girl go by between eight-thirty and eight-forty-five, last
Thursday morning. But it was unlikely that anyone would
have: this one doing breakfast dishes, that one making beds,
not looking idly out their front windows.

"Satan going up and down," said Piggott. "We haven't had
one of these in a while. That poor kid." It made you wonder
about bringing children into the world, he thought. When all
those predictions in Daniel looked like coming true pretty
soon. He'd been dating that nice girl Prudence—both of them
in the choir—but it made you wonder.

"Satan behind it all right, I guess," said Glasser. They went
up the front walk of the house on the corner. It was a big
frame place, originally a single house, now cut in half to make
two big apartments, two doors on the wide old-fashioned porch
across the front. Piggott put his finger on the bell of the right-

hand door. The slot above the mailbox had a dirty white paper strip in it labeled *Schultz*.

"Yeah?" A thin elderly man jerked open the door. Glasser recited their piece, introduced himself and Piggott. "Police? A kid? Don't know anything to say. Didn't see a damn thing myself. What? No, I don't live here alone. At a hundred a month? My daughter an' her husband live here too. Takes twenty-five a month o' my pension for the rent, that skinflint. What? They both work, be gone by eight o'clock in the morning."

Glasser thanked him politely and Piggott pushed the other bell. The strip in the slot above the mailbox there said *Sorenson*.

The old man cackled. "That won't do you no good. They're off up north, whole kit and caboodle of 'em. Pa 'n' Ma 'n' all the kids, five kids. His pa died and they all went up to Bakersfield for the funeral. Friday they went." He shut the door emphatically.

"You get discouraged sometimes, Henry," said Piggott.

"That's right, Matt. You sure do," said Glasser. "But at least we've got something new. We think. She came this way. Not back down Scott. So these people left Friday. I wonder when they'll be back. We ought to ask if anybody noticed her Thursday."

"So we'll have to check back." Piggott sighed. There were more places to try—the block along Montana opposite to the big school-ground: and it was early to knock off for lunch.

Mendoza and Hackett came into Federico's at twelve-thirty and found Higgins and Grace just before them; they sat down at one table and Higgins said gloomily that nothing more had showed for all the legwork. They hadn't turned up anybody else who'd seen Marla. "If you ask me, we've got all we're going to get on that. Forget it and start following up the pedigrees in Records. Bring me a Scotch and water, Adam, and the steak sandwich."

Hackett said in his usual martyred tone he'd have the low-calorie plate. "I'll go along with that, George. What the hell does it matter just where she was picked up? One thing sure, if anybody had seen it, they'd have said so. Then. You can talk about degenerated morals—*and* the Genovese case—all you want, a lot of that's so, but anybody who saw a child being forced into a car would call cops in a hurry. And nobody did. So nobody saw it."

"Yes," said Mendoza in a dissatisfied voice. "And you'd have thought she'd have had a chance to make some kind of fuss—scream, or—*lo digo y lo sostengo,* that damned book—" The waiter came back with his rye and Higgins' highball. Mendoza swallowed half the rye at once and turned on Grace. "You were working that García thing. What showed?"

"Nothing," said Grace placidly. "We'd better shove it in Pending. Which I do not like to do, but there are just no leads at all. I doubt very much that X intended to kill the woman, he was after the loot. The very small-time punk. When we pick up any of them who've been on the same lay, ask about Mrs. García—maybe some day we'll find him. But right now—" he shrugged.

"And there's Moreno and Romano," said Mendoza. *"Condenación.* I'm inclined to think that was this Rooney. The knife. The wide-bladed knife."

Landers came up and swung a chair round from a neighboring table; they made room for him. "Well, your little entrapment is set up," he told Mendoza. "Gabriel called Bessinger. That is the damndest thing—I mean, you'd think a four-year-old child would have better sense—walk up to a stranger and try to hire him to do a murder. He played it all right—Gabriel, I mean. I listened in. He's got a date to meet Bessinger at an address on Malabar at eight tonight. Bessinger sounded eager."

"Really. Address the one Goldberg's got for Bessinger?"

"No," said Landers. "The phone's in the name of a Ronald McFarley. And no, he's not in Records. Not ours, anyway."

Grace and Landers had an appointment set up with Marla's teacher. Carey and the other men would have seen her before, but just to question on facts. And because the disappearance of an eight-year-old would raise the natural suspicion of the pervert, they would have talked to some of the kids who knew Marla; but not, maybe, at any length. And Mendoza said if there was anything there to be got, their sweet-talker Grace would get it.

Grace didn't know about that. He could try. And use the empathy on it. Grace didn't know much about children: Virginia going to this specialist, they'd like a couple of their own.

The teacher, a Miss Grace Meade, was young and very distressed about Marla. "I know it's silly to feel it was my fault. But I can't help—The children don't usually take that book home, you see, and I was a little surprised that none of them *had* forgotten it, only Marla. And it was to teach her a little lesson about responsibility—But if I hadn't told her to go after it—! She was such a nice little girl, Mr. Grace." She divided a glance between them, tall boyish Landers and the dapper brown-faced Grace with his mustache as neat as Mendoza's.

"Oh, was she?" asked Grace gently. "A little shy? But normal intelligence?"

"Oh, I didn't mean that—no, she wasn't shy. At all. A nice little girl, and very intelligent. I'd say quite mature for her age. A—a level-headed child," said Miss Meade. "I can't understand how—some of them that age such innocents, the strangers coming up—but Marla wouldn't have."

They talked to the children in Marla's class. They talked to the younger sister Eileen, in second grade: a little pale white-rabbit of a blond child, more excited than grieved about Marla. Too young to know the real meaning of grief. She confirmed that she and Marla had gone to the Fosters' house after school last Wednesday—every day last week, like always. And there was cookies and milk, and sometimes if Mr. Foster came home early he played games with them and like that. She didn't remember anything about the book at all. None of the little girls in Marla's class could tell them anything about a strange man approaching her, or any of them. Most of them had been warned about strangers, and accepting rides in cars, and so on.

"Waste of time," said Landers. "I'm with George—look up

the pedigrees. Work it from that end." They had heard by
then about Piggott's brainstorm and Montana Street.

"I don't know," said Grace seriously. They had come over
here in his car, the little blue French racing Elva; he stood
dangling the keys in his hand, looking at the car abstractedly.
"I don't know, Tom. Level-headed, the teacher says. Well, that
means two different things maybe, an eight-year-old and a
grown-up. She meant level-headed for a kid that age. But how
did he get hold of her? On a city street down here?"

Landers took a last draw on his cigarette, dropped it, and
stepped on it. "Did you happen to see, Jase, a little while ago,
an article in that Sunday magazine by the fellow who tried
that experiment? In cooperation with some local force around
here, I forget if it was Glendale or Pasadena or whatever. The
experiment approaching the kids. First he tried it all slicked up
in clean clothes and shaved—respectable-looking. And then as
a bum, four-day beard and old clothes. Offering the candy, the
gum. And if you saw it, you'll remember that the majority of
the kids flocked around him both times, all eager. Forgetting
everything they'd ever been told about strangers and not accepting presents and so on. It was an eye-opener for him and
that force too. You've got to remember they're just kids,
Jase. . . . Look at them on bicycles."

"Bicycles?" said Grace.

"Boys on bicycles," said Landers, "I am terrified of. I tell
you. The damn bikes can swerve on a dime, *and* they do. And
I would take a bet that at least ninety percent of all parents
have said over and over again, Johnny, be careful on your bike,
remember to give signals, look where you're going, watch out
for cars. Ad infinitum. But do the kids remember? Swerve and
jink all over the place—delivering papers both sides of the
street, just riding around together—dash out in front of you,
no warning, you couldn't stop to save your life, even at twenty-
five m.p.h. They scare me. And if you hit one of 'em, it's all
your fault, poor little innocent."

"Well, I do see what you mean," said Grace thoughtfully.
"The kids . . ."

Mendoza dropped back to the office after lunch to see if there was anything new in. There was. "Lieutenant Goldberg just called," said Lake. "He's got one to hand over to us."

"Oh, hell," said Mendoza.

"He said he'd be in his office."

Mendoza went down to Goldberg's office. "As if I wasn't busy enough. So what have you got for us?"

"Don't blame me," said Goldberg. "I didn't do it. Sit down, I'll get you the file. We've had these punks wandering around pulling the holdups for a month or so. Nothing big, the neighborhood markets, variety stores, corner drugstores. They haven't got much anywhere. But the same descriptions on all the jobs, a little less here, a little more there—it adds up." He sneezed and groped for Kleenex. "It's all in our reports—three kids, sixteen, seventeen, with a gun. A big one maybe. They haven't—" he sneezed again. "Damn allergies." He dropped the Kleenex in the wastebasket. "So about twelve-thirty today they finally shoot off the gun and kill somebody. So you can go look for them for a change. I do swear, the kids these days—"

"*Pues sí*. And I suppose you haven't got any really useful leads at all."

"You read minds, Luis. Three punk kids, the ordinary clothes, the kind of descriptions you get from citizens? All I can tell you is, by what at least three witnesses say, one of them stutters."

"How helpful," said Mendoza. "Give me the file. I'll brood over it."

"And have a hunch." Goldberg sneezed.

"Not," said Mendoza, "on the wild punk kids, Saul. Be a fluke if we ever land on them. Who'd they shoot?"

"A William Blodgett. Clerk at a little general market over on Second Street. Man about fifty. There's a witness. She says Blodgett started to argue with them, the gun went off, and they all ran out. They didn't get a dime. You can do the legwork looking for witnesses outside. Once I saw he was dead, I just offered up a short prayer of thanks that I could turn it over to you." Goldberg brought out more Kleenex.

"I'll bet you did at that," said Mendoza. "Thanks for nothing."

"And what's all this about that Bill Bessinger?" Mendoza told him, and he sneezed, swore, said, "My God, people. None of the punks are very bright, or they wouldn't be punks, but you'd think anybody would have better sense—"

Mendoza went up to his office and read over the reports, did a little ruminating, and went out on that with Higgins. Both Higgins and Landers were off tomorrow; they'd be that much shorthanded.

And that book stayed at the back of his mind, damn it. He didn't know exactly what it was trying to say to him. They knew now that the book, Marla's schoolbook, had been at the Fosters'—the Pickens children's second home. She'd gone there to get it, she'd started back to school, she'd gone down to Montana instead of turning up Scott—Piggott the plodder did occasionally have a brainstorm—and then what? The book, not dropped until X had got Marla up there in the park, the nice quiet handy place—

Oh, yes?

It was funny. The word for it in Spanish—*extraño*. Funny-peculiar.

Higgins and Hackett had just come in together at five o'clock when a uniformed man delivered a manila envelope to Lake. The autopsy report on Marla. Bainbridge had got right on it; he knew they'd want whatever he could give them.

He didn't give them much. But among other things he gave them something funny.

She had been raped. She had been beaten, just with fists: no weapon used. But by a grown man, all right—severely beaten. Cause of death, manual strangulation; the hyoid bone in the throat fractured. But Marla had fought back, as well as she could. "Present in mouth, wedged in teeth, a strip of cloth one inch by approximately three-quarters of an inch, evidently bitten off in struggle. Cloth is a hundred percent cotton, tan in color, possibly from either shirt or trousers. Blood present in small quantity on cloth, analyzed, Type A-B." Marla was Type O.

"I will be damned," said Hackett. "A plucky kid. She bit him hard enough to draw blood. Maybe she's given us something."

"We have to find him before we can type his blood, Art," said Higgins. "Maybe the lab can get something more out of it." The cloth had been forwarded there. "Let's start looking at the ones out of Records. It's a place to start."

"And as Luis says," said Hackett, "tomorrow is also a day."

The Hollywood *Citizen-News* had its afternoon edition on the streets at two o'clock, with the first appearance of Alison's ad about Cedric.

Up to six-forty, when Mendoza came home, nobody at all had called to claim Cedric. He was still tied to the back railing, with a large aluminum bowl of water beside him, when Mendoza drove into the garage, and he got up and waggled his tailless rump in welcome. "So you're still here," said Mendoza. Cedric smiled at him and tossed his head to show his wild wall-eye. *"Dios,* what a man puts up with when he acquires a wife—not that I hold any brief for that pound—"

"No, nobody's called," said Alison. "But it's early, after all. Somebody *must*—Dinner in ten minutes, if you want a drink—"

"Nada. The offspring?"

"Having their baths. It's really pathetic, Luis, how he tries to make up to the cats. Bast clawed him when he tried to wash her, and he just looked surprised and backed off. And he's marvelous with the twins—"

"Somebody," said Mendoza, "will call. Whoever owns the idiot monster."

"Well, I hope so," said Alison.

He went down to the nursery bathroom and into the middle of strenuous argument from the offspring.

"Why *cann* Cedric come inside? *¡Perro lindo!* Bast 'n' Sheba 'n' Nefertite 'n' El Señor inside! Why *cann—?"*

"Now, Johnny, Cedric doesna belong to us, my boyo—don't fret now—" Máiri's comforting murmur.

"Nice Cedric. Daddy say Cedric stay," said Terry confidently, stark-naked in the tub. "Sheba a bad cat, put claws in

Cedric—nice Cedric. He licked my nose, 'n' *Mamacíta* says like kissing. Cedric—"

"Now, *mo croidhe,* into fresh pyjamas—"

"Daddy *say?*" said Terry insistently. "Cedric stay!"

"*¡Bueno! ¡Muy bien!*" said Johnny with immense satisfaction.

"Now, my dearies, someone will be missing the nice beastie and worrying, the same as we'd be were Bast or Sheba lost— not ours he is—*Out* we come, Terry—"

"*¡Caray!*" said Mendoza.

"They can't think about anything else," said Mrs. Mac-Taggart, looking harassed. "That dog—"

"Will not be here long," said Mendoza. Females! Wives! That moronic lost dog—Not that he would say, the pound. After *all*. He knew how he'd feel if Bast or any of them was lost—the idiotic creature must belong somewhere, and eventually someone would see the ad.

Chapter Four

"I DON'T know as I feel just go good about this," said Loveluck uneasily. "I feel kind of nervous, Detec——"

"Now for God's sake," said Landers, "relax. And don't say detective. We're going to try to get him to do most of the talking. Just relax, you'll be O.K. We do appreciate your helping us out, you know. Come on."

The little praise seemed to steady Loveluck. They went up to the porch of the little square duplex in silence. "He said the left side—"

"O.K., let's go." Landers reached up and switched on the miniature microphone concealed in the breast pocket of his ancient plaid sport-shirt. He had on old brown slacks and scuffed moccasins to match Loveluck's tan shirt and pants.

The door opened halfway to show only a dim light inside. "That you?—uh, who's *that?*" The shadow in the door shied back, and Landers nudged Loveluck.

"Oh, you don't need to be nervous—it's a pal o' mine, he's O.K.—I'm not just so sure about this deal yet, he says if I decide not to he might take it on for you. He's O.K."

"Oh. Well—come in." They went in, and the door shut, and after a minute an overhead light came on. As easy as that, marveled Landers. He looked at Bessinger.

"Is that the guy, Bill?" A woman came into the shabby square living room, looking anxious. She was about thirty, a bit plump, a bleached blonde in purple hostess pyjamas. "Hey, I thought you said one guy."

"Yeah, yeah," said Bessinger. He looked at Landers searchingly.

"He's O.K., I tell you," said Loveluck. "He's—uh—got a lot more experience than me. With—with guns and so on. He said—"

"He got a name maybe?"

"What's names got to do with it?" said Landers roughly. "You got a job you want done, I heard."

"Well," said Bessinger, licking his lips, "well, hell, so long as it's done I don't care who does it, God knows." He was a stocky red-haired man with quick-moving little light eyes and a weak chin with a dimple in it. "So long as the dame can't testify at the trial—or ever, that's all. So long as she's took off."

"You said a grand," said Loveluck. "For doing it. For taking her off. What's her name again?"

"Spears. Naomi Spears. Jeanie, get us some beer, hah? Siddown," said Bessinger. "I give you her address, you do it however you want."

"The money first," said Landers. They had to play one like this very carefully, to avoid the actual legal entrapment.

"Uh, well, the money," said Bessinger. "I tell you how it is. I—my brother-in-law, see, this is his place, see, Jeanie's my sister—he's been helping me try to raise the money. I got three hundred I can give you now, that's about it. If you'd—Jeanie, is Ron back yet? He said he could maybe raise another couple hundred from—"

She came in with three bottles of beer on a tray. "You ain't heard him drive in, have you? No." She had a loud nasal voice; it ought to come over well on the miniature tape, Landers thought. She put her hands on her plump hips, looking at him and Loveluck. "Look, we'll raise the dough—honest, you guys. You take the three centuries now, we won't renege. You'll get the rest of it O.K."

"Sure, sure!" said Bessinger. "Look, I tell you confidentially, see, I could get it for you tomorrow if the damn fuzz was off my neck. I hid some of the loot I got on that last job, only do I know if the damn fuzz maybe know it and have a tail on me? See? But once that dame's out of the way, they ain't got a leg to stand on at the trial. I get off and then I can—You don't need to worry. I—I even get you a gun if you need one. To take her off."

"I don't know," said Landers doubtfully. "Make it five, maybe we'll think about it."

"Jesus, you got to!" said Bessinger. "I got to get rid o' that dame! I never knew nothing about that law, it was that shyster the judge appointed me said about it—I never *heard* o' such a thing, talk about police state and all, jeez, it ain't as if I done a murder!" He looked aggrieved and scared.

"I didn't figure it could be right, but we got Ron to ask a lawyer he knows and it *is*," said the blonde. "Something about, third count on a felony, you can get *life*. This state. My God—"

"Yeah, yeah, so you see I got to get rid o' that dame," said Bessinger urgently. "Come on, you guys, I positively guarantee you the rest of it, you take the three hundred now and—"

Landers got up. "You got to do a little better than that, punk," he said harshly. "Make it half and we'll think about it." Loveluck was at the door ahead of him.

"Please—" Bessinger almost wailed. He followed them out to the porch. "I'll get it! I promise you—same time tomorrow night, here, hah? I'll have it, Ron can raise it somehow—honest—"

"D-did you get what you wanted?" asked Loveluck in the car.

"I think enough for our purpose," said Landers, "yes. You were fine, Mr. Loveluck, we appreciate the cooperation." He was thinking that, desperate as Bessinger sounded, it might not be a bad idea to put a couple of patrolmen to watch over Mrs. Spears until the warrant came through.

"Oh. I—I thought you didn't seem very pleased about it."

Landers laughed a little cynically. "That was really amusing in a way. He'd never heard of that statute before. A third felony charge, you can get life. The little joker there is, Mr. Loveluck, which Bessinger apparently doesn't know, that when you get a life sentence in California, you'll be eligible for parole in just seven years."

He took Loveluck home, went back to the office, listened to the tape with the night men Galeano and Schenke, and called Mendoza. "I think we've got some nice self-incriminating evidence. The sister and brother-in-law are in on it too."

"*Bueno*," said Mendoza. "We'll apply for the warrant in the morning."

"A kind of tentative meeting set up, same time and place, tomorrow night. If the warrant comes through by then you'll know where to find 'em."

"Thanks so much."

"And what about protection for Mrs. Spears until we do?"

"Just to be on the safe side. Yes."

Nobody at all had called to claim Cedric by the time Mendoza left for the office on Wednesday morning. As he backed out the Ferrari he had a last glimpse of Cedric hopefully waggling his hairy rump at Bast, who was sitting feet folded under her just out of range, staring remotely over Cedric's head.

Higgins and Landers were off. Mendoza borrowed a couple of men from Traffic to set up the protection on Mrs. Spears. The legwork down there on Marla's route, asking the questions, might still yield a little something, but had likely already given them everything of importance; it was now more imperative to start looking for the possibles out of Records. They had a list of forty-six men to hunt for and question, and he and Hackett and Palliser divided them up and started out in the mild February weather on the hunt. Mendoza sent up the formal application for the warrant on Bessinger and the McFarleys. Conspiracy to commit homicide-first. The tape had turned out nice and clear.

They'd have handed over some of the list to Grace and Piggott too; somebody had to stay in to mind the store and take whatever new calls came in, and Glasser looked like being it today; but at eight-forty, just as Mendoza was about to hand over some names and take off himself, they got the first new call of the day, and it looked like being one of those with a lot of paperwork and fuss, so he sent Grace and Piggott out on it and set out to cover his part of the list.

Frederick Emmett, now fifty-six, a record back to 1933. Indecent exposure, attempted molestation, attempted rape, forcible rape of minor. He'd served fifteen years on the last charge, was out of Quentin two years and still on parole. Address on Thirty-fourth Street. And that just the first one.

It was the father who had called in. A Richard Wheeler, address on New Hampshire just beyond Vermont, a middle-class quiet area of small apartments and single homes. Wheeler was, they instantly decided, in a state of shock: outwardly just incoherent, but they'd both seen that before. A rather handsome man in the late forties, dark hair, a good jaw, and his eyes frighteningly blank.

"But I was just having breakfast—an ordinary day—didn't believe it when the boy told me—until I looked—don't believe it, I can't believe it, always such a good youngster, Dicky, only nineteen, but my God, my God, so was—*was*—he said—but *Dicky!* I'm sorry, I'm not explaining myself clearly to you, I'm sorry, my name's Wheeler, I've got a card here somewhere, Western representative of Purcell and Mack, locks, you know, keys and safes and—"

Grace looked at Piggott, who found a phone in the hall of this tidy, well-furnished, well-appointed house, and called an ambulance. And the boy—not a boy, of course, thought Grace, nineteen—sat quietly on the couch and stared at the floor. He was a good-looking young man, tall and well built like his father, good features without being handsome; and he was neat and clean in white shirt and dark slacks. He didn't seem to hear his father's loud gabbling voice; by the time the ambulance came, a hysterical voice. The interns gave the father a shot and took him away, and Grace sat down beside Dicky Wheeler and said, "You told your father about it—you like to tell us?"

He raised dark eyes to Grace's dark eyes. His expression was blank. He said, "I don't know why I did it. Well, in a kind of way I do. She'd gone out with other guys. And I—and

I—thought she was my girl. Mine. We had a fight about it—last night, before we went to the movies. She said—she said she didn't belong to anybody—and she'd go out with whoever she wanted. And I was mad about it—and after—after, we got to fighting again, I mean just talking, you know, and that's when I—I don't *remember,* kind of, like it was all a dream after —but I *do* remember in a kind of way—" He was clenching and unclenching his fists, staring at the floor. Piggott was standing watching him, his thin dark face expressionless. "And—then I must have just driven home and come in—and cleaned up—and gone to bed, only when I woke up there was all my clothes with the blood—and I—and I went and looked in the car and I thought maybe—put her somewhere—hide—but it was *Pat,* and I—then—I just thought I'd better tell Dad—" He began to cry suddenly. "I don't know why I did it."

Piggott went out to the garage and looked. Two cars, a Pontiac sedan and a two-door Ford. In the back seat of the Ford was the beaten and bloody corpse of a young woman. The I.D. in the handbag on the floor said she was Patricia Desmond, address up in Hollywood, Normandie Avenue. Piggot called downtown for another ambulance, and they waited until it came, and the mobile-lab truck, and then took Dicky Wheeler back to the office.

Punctiliously they told him about all his rights, and asked him if he wanted a lawyer. He just shook his head; but they got one there anyway, from the Public Defenders' office, before they got his confession down on paper. These days they had to tie it all up really tight to be sure it wouldn't be thrown out on some technicality.

At ten o'clock, when Grace and Glasser were still discussing it with the lawyer, before starting to get the confession down, Piggott drove up to Hollywood to break the news to the girl's family. Which was a part of the thankless job he detested, but it had to be done. It was, he thought as he drove, the utter senselessness of so much of what they ran into these days, that got you. As if the devil had all of a sudden succeeded in removing all common sense from a cross-section of the population. Or, reflected Piggott gloomily, his representatives here below: of which there were all too many. The new morality hardly new: it used to be called sin.

The address was one of those new own-your-own-apartments. Big places: apartments as big as some houses. The woman who came to the door was still pretty, in her forties, slim and dark, and dressed in street clothes, a flowered hat in one hand. "Yes?"

"Mrs. Desmond? I'm Detective Piggott, L.A.P.D." He showed her the badge.

She looked bewildered. "Police? What do you want here?"

"I'm afraid I've got some bad news for you, ma'am. Your daughter Patricia—Is your husband here? Any other member of the family?"

"Why, no. Jim just left for the office. Pat?" She smiled. "She's still asleep—I didn't wake her. She was out with that nice Wheeler boy last night, and she must have been late, I didn't hear her come in. But no reason to get her up, she's not—What *do* you mean?"

Piggott hated this job. But somebody—"Mrs. Desmond," he began, "I'm afraid she isn't here. She's—"

In the end he had to call an ambulance for her too; and then try to locate the husband. It all occupied most of the morning, and there'd be mounds of paperwork on it, the arraignment, the inquest, trial, or hearing: how many thousands of the taxpayers' dollars laid out, and how much grief for the innocent people, just because of—well, you could take your choice between evil and stupidity, but on this one the balance came down a little heavier on stupidity. Which was a commodity also much used by Satan.

Higgins got up a little later than usual and after breakfast went out to cut the lawn. Mary was back from driving the kids to school then: usually she wouldn't indulge them, but with Stevie's brace—She was mixing up a cake when Higgins came in about nine-thirty after fixing that loose latch on the driveway gate. The little Scottie, Brucie, came in with him and flopped at their feet.

"It's just, damn it, you can't help worrying," said Higgins.

"When you see a thing like this. That poor Pickens kid. The innocent ones. I know Laura's been told, I know she's a good kid ordinarily. But it *happens*."

"You can't keep them hermetically sealed off, George. Forever. Protected all the way. They've got to learn."

"I know that too, damn it."

"All you can do, really," said Mary, "is try to teach them good principles, instill some morality into them—right and wrong—and hope enough will stick to protect them."

"I know, I know. But you can't help worrying."

"Well, no," she said. "No."

"I've been wondering—" said Higgins. What he wondered about was Echo Park. There Marla had been, on her way back to school, just a couple of blocks from the park, with its lake and boats and swans—the lake visible from where she'd been. Had Marla, just possibly, on impulse decided to play hookey —thinking, only a little while—and gone down to the park? There wouldn't have been many people around there, on a weekday morning. And what was in his mind was that it would have been a great deal easier for the pervert to pick her up in the park. The careful friendly approach—"The swans are pretty, aren't they?" Not the crude grab. So the inexperienced, unjudging child (warned or not) responded, not at all alarmed. That might have been very easy indeed—if she'd been in the park.

He drove down there about ten-thirty. It was a slightly overcast morning, the sun trying to break through: a mild, nice day. Hardly anyone in the park, as he'd thought. A handful of people, mostly elderly people, sitting around on the benches. Most people would be at work, children at school. He'd come down into the park on the side of the lake where Marla would have come, opposite the boathouse and little sandwich stand. Five people visible here, all at a distance from each other, sitting on the benches, the grass: one old woman knitting rapidly with flashing needles.

Higgins asked all of them if they had been in the park last Thursday morning. Two of the women had, but neither remembered a little girl in a light-blue dress.

Which didn't say she hadn't been here. He still thought it

was an idea. There were trees, big shrubs, the benches not all visible from each other. And how very easy to strike up the friendly conversation with an innocent little girl in this green, quiet, friendly place where the great white swans floated lazily on the blue water and the ducks busily upended themselves after the bottom weeds.

He looked at the lake, remembering that body in it last year, and his mouth tightened. A lot of legwork, the tiresome routine, on this one. And other things doubtless showing up.

He didn't know but what he'd drop into the office to see what was going on.

Mendoza, Hackett, and Palliser landed back at the office together just before noon with two of the more likely-looking suspects out of Records to question. Mendoza had Harvey Evans, forty-two, five convictions of exposure, attempted molestation, attempted rape, still on parole. Hackett and Palliser had Charles Poole, twenty-nine, a very similar record, just released from Camarillo into custody of his parents.

"Take a quick look before lunch," said Mendoza, hunching his shoulders at Poole, who was a shaggy-haired, sullen-looking lout in unkempt clothes.

"I just wonder," said Hackett, "if the head-doctors ever *think*, Luis. Just plain straightforward thinking. Released in custody of his parents. They must know something about the parents? In this case, Poole Senior has a pedigree too—petty theft mostly—and the mother's a lush. What I mean is—"

"Yes," said Mendoza. "I sometimes wonder too."

And the phone rang on Sergeant Lake's desk. Lake picked it up and after a moment beckoned Hackett. "A shy pigeon who won't talk to anybody but you."

"If it was anybody else, flattering . . . Hackett. Oh. Oh, you don't say. The what? Giuseppi's, yes, I've got that. O.K., I'll see you're taken care of, Joe." He put the phone down, looking annoyed. "That Rooney. One of our pet pigeons just spotted him over at a bar on Main. I suppose we'd better—"

"You are so right," said Mendoza. "Henry can sit in with

me on one of these boys." Grace and Piggott were still busy on the Wheeler thing.

"After all," said Palliser as they started off again, "Rooney is very possible for Moreno and Romano, and we'd like to get those cleared up, Art."

"Granted, granted," said Hackett. But he had an orderly mind, and it always annoyed him to have to leave one thing and jump to another thing, and then back to something else. But that was what they were doing most of the time.

Giuseppi's bar on Main, not quite on the Row but not far from it, was a dark hole in the wall, redolent of beer, sweat, stale food, and too much unwashed humanity. They stopped in the entrance, letting their eyes become accustomed to the dim light; there were only a few people in the place, all men.

"Over there in the corner," muttered Palliser. "Is it?"

Hackett peered. "Looks like him," he said with satisfaction. Interruption or no, it was always gratifying to drop on the wanted man. And with one like Rooney, thereby saving God knew how much misery and death and grief to the innocents. He had a bad record, Rooney. They knew he'd done three rape-murders: how many more he'd done, and other things, only God knew too.

They walked quietly over to where he sat alone at a table, hunched over a glass, and it was Palliser who showed the badge. That, they didn't have to rehearse; it was automatic. Rooney was six-three, a hundred and ninety, only twenty-two, and known to be a mean one. And while Palliser stood six feet, Rooney had twenty pounds on him; but Hackett more than matched Rooney in height, and outweighed him.

"We're taking you in, Rooney," said Palliser quietly.

The big man looked up slowly, and down to the badge in Palliser's hand. He said muzzily, "Fuzz. Goddamn—" And rose up suddenly, overturning the table with a crash. He hit Palliser left-handed, a solid chop across the neck, and Palliser fell, caught himself on the table, and was up. Hackett grabbed Rooney's shoulder, hauled him round, and belted him hard on the jaw. Rooney's head snapped back, but he came on, drove head down for Hackett's stomach, and fell on him as Hackett went down. Palliser fell on top and tried to drag him up. Hackett heaved up, got to his knees, shoved Rooney away and hit him again. Rooney staggered to his feet at the same time Hackett got up, and got in a lucky blow while Hackett was off-balance. He was swearing at the top of his voice all the while.

Hackett went down again, and Palliser tried a judo chop at Rooney's neck. It didn't quite come off. Rooney turned, snarling, got hold of Palliser's jacket, and yanked, tearing off half his jacket and shirt; then he lunged for Palliser's throat and nearly sent him over backward. "Art!" panted Palliser. "Are you—?"

Hackett hoisted himself to his feet, got hold of Rooney, pulled him off Palliser, and hit him on the jaw again. Rooney, still swearing, charged at Hackett—and then suddenly his feet went out from under him and he was falling. Hackett dodged, but was carried over backward, half under Rooney, who lay very still.

Palliser straightened painfully and felt his jaw. "Art? You all right? Is he—?"

Hackett got up again, slowly. "Whoosh," he said. "I must be getting old, John. If he hadn't slipped in his own beer he knocked over—" He was going to have a beautiful black eye, by the feel, and assorted other damage—his shirt was ripped, and he'd twisted one knee, and he was still trying to catch his breath. Age, undoubtedly. Thirty-seven to twenty-two. "You all right?"

"More or less," said Palliser.

Rooney was out cold, of his own weight hitting the floor. The six other people in the place, only the bartender standing, were all watching. Just watching. One man spat on the floor and mumbled, "Cops. Hit, hit, break the head in. Guy just sittin' there." They had all seen Rooney start the fight; but that was another aspect of the thankless job.

"Ambulance," said Hackett. "We can't take him in like that. All the rights. Thank God it's J. Edgar who wants him. Not up to us to make the charge."

"No. Not even if he is X on Moreno and Romano—they've got a prior charge."

They saw Rooney taken off, and went back to the office to report, and then they both went home to change their clothes and patch up injuries.

"Well!" said Angel as Hackett came in the back door. "And what did you do in the great war, Daddy? Are you all *right?* What happened now?" She turned off the electric beater, looking concerned.

"We got that Rooney. Only he nearly got me first. I'm getting old, my Angel." He made for the bedroom. Mark dashed in from the backyard to greet Daddy home early. Sheila, who had just belatedly discovered how to walk after a fashion, came to meet him as drunkenly as any candidate for A.A., holding up demanding arms.

"That shirt's ruined, Art. Your eye—"

"Well, at least we've got him. Have we got any aspirin?"

When she brought him the aspirin and a glass of water, she asked, "Anything new on that poor child?"

"I don't think so. It's slow, one like that. But please God we'll get him too."

"Well!" said Roberta as Palliser came in. "What does the other fellow look like? What on *earth,* John—"

"That Rooney. He's out cold in the emergency hospital."

"My hero."

"But if Art Hackett hadn't been along, it'd probably be me in the ambulance. I suppose you can use this shirt for washing windows or something—" but at the look in her eyes, above her determined smile, he hugged her and said, "It doesn't really happen often, you know. To ranking plainclothesmen."

"Once can be enough. All right, I'm not fussing," said Roberta.

Nobody had called about the ad at all. "I can't understand it," said Alison. "He's got to belong somewhere. A purebred dog, the doctor said, and somebody's pet, the tag and all."

"It could be if you put an ad in the *Times, achara*—not everybody will see the Hollywood paper—"

"Yes, I think I'd better. I would have to begin with, only I naturally thought—*And*," said Alison, "when somebody does claim him it's going to be *murder* with the twins, *Máiri*. The way they've fallen in love with him—and he is a darling."

"It canna be helped. The beastie belongs somewhere."

"I'll call the *Times*. Maybe if I put, *seems to like cats*, the owner would spot it easier."

So that was that, thought Sergeant Barth of Wilcox Street, leaning back. All the paperwork on the latest freeway crash. And a pity: a whole family wiped out.

It was funny about that dog. That Mrs. Ruggles had said positively, a dog. No sign of a dog. Oh, well, an academic matter. If the dog had been hurt, it'd have been found by now; a stray dog would be picked up by the pound eventually. . . .

Bast coiled her tail more tightly around her and considered the stranger. As the senior cat, and mother, it was obviously up to her to evaluate him.

She was puzzled about him, and had only halfway made up her mind. It had seemed at first that he was, obviously, Dog. The hated one. But he did not behave like Dog. He tried to wash her, he did no chasing, he made no retaliation to claws or hissings, and Nefertite had stolen his food under his nose while he only watched and tried to wash *her*. It was cats who washed cats. He smelled like Dog, but he could not be.

But what was he? Bast tucked her front feet under her and watched him steadily. He stretched on his rope and reached to lick her ruddy Abyssinian nose. *Friends,* he said, but Bast was cautious. If not Dog, what was he?

Chapter Five

HIGGINS drifted into the office just as Hackett had arrived back. "What the hell are you doing here?" asked Hackett.

"I hadn't much of anything to do, and I just wondered if you'd turned up anything. And where'd you get the shiner?"

Hackett felt his eye, which was indeed developing nicely. "Rooney," he said briefly. Palliser came in, limping slightly, in a clean white shirt and a different suit. "And if you really want to do some overtime, we can use you, all right—"

"Say it twice," said Mendoza behind him. He looked a trifle harried. "We haven't done one damned thing on those punks Goldberg handed us. John, if you feel up to it will you look over Goldberg's file on that and chase over there and see if you can turn up any more witnesses? Ballistics ought to give us something on the gun, I should hope. Are you just feeling dedicated, George?"

"That's me."

"Well, we can always use more help. I got nothing out of Poole before I knocked off for lunch, but we'll talk to him some more. This and that came up—Henry and Matt went out on the suicide, and the new D.O.A. over on the Row will have to wait. Jase is still coping with the paperwork on Wheeler—we got the father down to identify the body formally—"

"That thing," said Hackett.

"Another new one?" said Higgins.

They brought him up to date on that. "No mystery—we do so seldom get the mystery—but tiresome."

"Well, I had a thought," said Higgins. "Echo Park." He outlined the little idea, and Mendoza looked interested.

"De acuerdo—si será cierto. You're right, of course, a hell of a lot easier to pick her up there. Just get into the casual talk. Even the little girl warned about strangers—the friendly stranger admiring the swans with her wouldn't be a stranger in that sense. But against it, George, I'll remind you that by all we've got Marla was a conscientious, responsible little girl. Ordinarily. Would she have played hookey? Even for a little while? She'd got her book and was heading back for school."

"I don't know," said Higgins. "Who knows what an eight-year-old would do? Impulse—it was just an idea."

"And we'll keep it in mind," said Mendoza. "But right now, let's talk to the two birds in hand." Palliser had gone out with Goldberg's file.

They continued to get nothing out of Poole. He sat silent and sullen, head down, and growled at them. Poole was young enough that he knew all about his rights and the rules hamstringing the fuzz.

"Do you remember where you were last Thursday morning?"

"No."

"Were you anywhere down here?"

"No. I don't hafta say nothing to you."

"You see the stories in the paper about the little girl murdered?"

"I don't know nothing about it."

It went like that, and Poole was really all up in the air anyway. It would probably be impossible to establish an alibi for him. He was just, like all the rest out of Records, a possible. Only a couple of those from Records they were hunting had actually done murder in the course of raping a minor; to the credit of the courts, despite all the laxness these days, child murder did still draw the stiff sentences. But any pervert was the potential killer. Poole was impossible to do anything with, as some would be; nothing said yes or no on him. They let him go, and brought in Harvey Evans.

Evans was a different matter. He was an older man, he had a longer pedigree. He was an insignificant-looking little man, sitting there between the twin looming bulks of Hackett and Higgins; a little thin man, neatly dressed in old blue slacks and a white shirt. He had a string of arrests and minor sentences for indecent exposure, attempted solicitation of minors, one attempted rape. He was on parole for that, lived with his elderly mother, and worked part time at a newsstand.

"You remember what you were doing last Thursday morning, Harvey?" Hackett.

He blinked. "I—I'm not quite sure."

"Were you anywhere around Echo Park?"

"Well, maybe. Maybe I was."

"Did you see the newspaper stories about the little girl who was killed?" Higgins.

He nodded. "Oh, yes. I did."

"You like little girls, don't you, Harvey?"

Evans looked down at his hands clasped in his lap. He had a weak rabbity face and shifty small eyes. "Oh, yes, I do," he said in a trembling voice. "Yes. You know I do."

"Did you have anything to do with that, Harvey? With Marla?" He had been duly warned, the piece recited to him; it apparently hadn't meant much to him. He looked up at Mendoza, blinking rapidly.

"It's bad of me," he said. "I know it's a bad thing. I remember, the preacher always saying, confess your sins. I guess I got to do that. I guess it was me did that. Yes."

Higgins let out a long slow breath.

"So we'll hear about it, Harvey. Where did you meet her? Marla."

"Ah—why, on the street. I don't remember which street. Somewhere."

"And then what did you do?"

"I—ah—I asked if she'd go on a walk with me and she said yes, and so I took her—I took her along until we came to a—an empty lot, and there was this big billboard there and I got her to come behind it—so's nobody would see, you know"—he was talking faster and faster—"and when I first took hold of her she started to yell, so I had to keep her quiet, so I guess I hit her and—and then she was all quiet and I thought soon as she come to she could tell everybody it was me, so I—so then I took this knife I had in my pocket and I cut her throat with it. And—and I'm sorry for what I did. It was bad."

He looked up at them anxiously for approval. "I see," said Mendoza. "And then what, Harvey?"

"I—uh, then I went home. That's all."

"All right," said Mendoza. They moved across the room.

"Another nut," said Higgins disgustedly.

"Not that I think Harvey's so smart," said Hackett, "but I've often thought that'd be a very cute way to get away with murder, Luis. Come tearing down to confess to every homicide five years running—don't we get them, the nuts?—and so when you come eagerly confessing to one you really did, we wouldn't even listen."

"But Harvey's not that smart," disagreed Mendoza. He went back to Harvey and told him he could go home.

"But I just said I did it—honest, I—"

"You think about it some more," said Mendoza; and Evans stumbled out, head down.

Sergeant Lake poked his head in. "There's a Fed here. On Rooney."

They came out to find it was Bright. "Congratulations, and thanks so much for Rooney. A good one to have out of circulation. With any luck he'll get the chair. I heard that you thought he might have been up to something here."

"We'd like to know yes or no," said Mendoza. "Two rape-murders. Looked very much like a couple he'd done before, elsewhere. The knife used, and—"

"Oh, really," said Bright. "Well, if it's any use to you, there was a knife on him when the hospital undressed him—he's got concussion, by the way—and you're welcome to it, here it is. Maybe your lab can say yes or no, and put your mind at rest, Lieutenant."

"Oh, *muy lindo*," said Mendoza to the knife in its plastic bag. It was a long wood-handled knife with an unusually wide blade; an old, much-used knife. "Bainbridge did say a wide blade. Thanks so much."

"Glad to oblige. Hope it does you some good," said Bright genially.

The new suicide was depressing. Piggott and Glasser looked at it superficially, because it was a very obvious suicide and there wasn't much point in prodding deeper. The interns waited to be told they could have the corpse.

An old lady, Martha Grimes, in a shabby room in a rooming house on Banning Street. An old lady without quite enough to live on, a sick old lady who knew she wasn't going to get well, with no relations and no friends. She had carefully piled towels at the base of the door, and shut the window, and turned the gas heater on full. The landlady had found her; they'd had to wait a while to look around, until the gas had dissipated.

"I don't know, Henry," said Piggott, "ordinarily I don't approve of suicide, but there are times I could think the Lord forgives it."

"Maybe, Matt, maybe. Anyway, there's nothing here for us but the paperwork," said Glasser, and added to the interns, "you can take her."

"Did you get a good look at them?" asked Palliser. "Could you describe any of them?"

Mrs. Amelia Lowry drew a long pleasurable breath. And Palliser made due allowance, knowing this and that about human nature. It hadn't really pleased Mrs. Lowry to witness the killing of a fellow human being, but it had put her suddenly in the limelight, she was important, her name would be in the papers, and she was being asked by the police, those august upright men (Mrs. Lowry being one of the citizens who still thought of them that way), for help. "Oh, yes!" she said proudly. "Yes, I can!" She looked at Palliser eagerly, a fat dowdy woman in an old but clean cotton housedress, run-over shoes: a round-faced, middle-aged woman with untidy gray-brown hair and oddly young-looking blue eyes. "I got good eyesight, I can tell you all about it. It was terrible—"

"You went into the market about noon?" Goldberg's man hadn't taken a formal statement from her, knowing it would be turned over to Homicide.

"Yes, I'd forgot coffee and Fred—my husband—he's always home for lunch. I trade there a lot, Mr. Blodgett was a nice friendly man, and obliging, you know. It was terrible! Fred's often said to me how his boss—Fred, he works at a Union station over on Olympic—always tells him, Fred, the holdup guy shows, give him the money, don't argue, it's not worth getting shot. And that's *so*. Because it was because Mr. Blodgett—but my goodness, Mr.—did you say Palliser?—I can see why he would, on account they were just *kids*. Just kids. Didn't look more'n fifteen to me, sixteen at the outside. Awful. What kids get up to these days, you can't hardly believe it, can you? I tell you my two wasn't raised like that—and they never got in no trouble, neither. Both married and doing well—But I get off the track. I'd just come in, and Mr. Blodgett said Good morning, and I says was there any coffee on special sale, when they come in. These kids. There wasn't nobody else in the market right then, and at first I thought—and I suppose so did Mr. Blodgett—they was after candy or pop or some such. Anyways, he was just saying Harvest Day was on special, sixty-nine cents, when these kids come pushing right up and I saw the gun. A gun—I never saw a gun so close as that, Mr. Palliser—"

"The kids. Could you—?"

"—and saying about a holdup. I didn't believe it. I thought for a minute, honest, it was a kid's joke, the way little boys have a toy pistol and say bang-bang—you know. I guess Mr. Blodgett thought so too. Anyways he says, you wait your turn, sonny, and he reaches up to the shelf for my coffee, and then one of the kids says real loud, Didn't you hear what we said, Mister? This is a holdup—and Mr. Blodgett turned around and right then the gun went off—" She stopped for breath. "It was *awful*, he just sort of grabbed himself and slid down real slow behind the counter—"

"Mrs. Lowry, could you give me any kind of description of them?"

"Yes, Mr. Palliser, I can. I guess it's as if the whole picture got kind of printed on my brain. I'll never forget it. They was all about the same age, not more'n sixteen, and two of 'em were about of a size—scrawny kids, not very big, maybe about as tall as me—I'm five-five—but a lot thinner." Momentarily she smiled, and sobered. "And one of them, he stuttered. I don't know if he stutters all the time, maybe he was excited, but he stuttered then. He said, stuttering like, you know, 'Oh, gee, H-Harry, why'd you d-do that?' That was just before they run out. And the third one, the one had the gun, he was bigger. He was maybe five-foot-eight, maybe not quite so much, and fatter too, but not fat. A big kid for that age, just as young as the others, you could tell. He had on boots and brown pants and a pink shirt—the other two just had on jeans and like sport-shirts, colored."

"That's very good, thanks," said Palliser. "They were all white, not Negro?"

"Yes, sir. The big one, I remember him best, he had a kind of round face, and blondy like hair, not real blond, but light brown, and a real high voice."

"Thanks very much," repeated Palliser. That was helpful; she was a good witness. And it jibed with what Goldberg had got from other witnesses on the other little jobs these punks had pulled, where nobody had been killed, over the last six weeks or so. It tied up. Three kids, two about of a size, one bigger. One stuttering. They hadn't got much loot: they'd hit an independent drugstore, a couple of other markets, a sandwich bar. But, over a fairly wide area. And just how did you go looking for them?

First of all, thought Palliser, look at the records of the under-eighteens. The j.d.'s they couldn't fingerprint, but who'd been up to this and that deviltry.

They might just be there. If not, try the public high schools—junior highs. Three kids, such and such descriptions, who ran together.

You had to start some place.

At four-forty, just as Hackett had fetched in another one out of Records to lean on, Sergeant Lake hurried into the interrogation room looking excited. "Call from the desk downstairs—your rapist's been caught, over on Baxter Drive—trying to pick up a kid—couple of neighbors holding him, they called in and a squad car's on the way. The desk—"

Mendoza, Hackett, and Higgins leaped up. "Address?" snapped Mendoza, snatching for his hat. Higgins felt the shoulder holster absently. Lake read off the address, and they plunged for the elevator down the hall.

"Baxter," said Mendoza as they rode down, fuming with impatience. "*Por Dios,* yes, that's only fifteen, eighteen blocks from Montana, Scott—the same area." He had encyclopedic knowledge of the sprawling city. "By God, are we going to get a break on this? By God—" He ran for the Ferrari in the lot, and the two big men squeezed in after him, Hackett in the passenger's seat, Higgins precarious in the jump-seat behind. The twelve-cylinder engine roared to life. "By God, I'll have a siren put on this thing before I'm a week older—Baxter, off Allesandro up there this side of the Glendale freeway—*Por Dios,* it could be we've got a break, the citizens sometimes useful—"

Little narrow residential streets up this way, past Echo Park: old streets, a few new with the jerry-built boxes of houses. The brakes complained as Mendoza swung the Ferrari around narrow corners, avoiding the lights and stationary stops, and turned into Baxter Street twelve minutes after they'd piled into the car.

"There's the squad car," said Higgins. The black-and-white patrol car sat up there at the end of the block, in front of a white-painted bungalow; one front door of the car hung open. People had come out on front lawns, the sidewalk, staring up there curiously. Mendoza pulled up behind the squad car, and they all piled out and ran up the walk of the house. The front door was open behind a screen door, and a woman was talking rapidly in a loud voice. Mendoza jerked open the screen door.

"—knew it must be *him,* this *monster* who murdered that other poor child—poor Geraldine was *terrified,* God knows

I've warned her, and after that terrible thing happened, just last night I told her all over again—oh, thank God she got away from him! And that *creature,* she pointed him out to me, just walking down the street there right in front of our house—and I knew—"

"Yes, ma'am, if you'd just relax and slow down—" One of the uniformed men attempting to soothe her. The other one was standing grimly over a little tableau at the other end of this shabby if orderly living room: a big bald elderly man and a big muscular young man hanging onto the arms of a third man seated in a straight chair—one on each side of him, looking angry and triumphant.

"—knew Mr. Herkimer was home next door, and Bill too, and I just *screamed.* A creature like that—murdering that poor sweet child—and goodness knows how many others—I've warned Geraldine about them, any strange man—you never know—and they came right over and I told them, this terrible monster, there he was right down the street—and they—"

"He put up a fight, all right," said the older man, with a grim smile, "but we took him, Bill and me. Devil like this, pickin' up the innocent little kids—we got him for you!" He blew on one knuckle, looking pleased.

Mendoza brought up short, looking at the captive. Who raised his head and asked, "Are you police? Honest-to-God police?"

"Sir, he tried to—but the young fellow hit him and I had to stop that—" said the first uniformed man.

"Yes, we're police," said Mendoza. "Honest-to-God police."

The man had been considerably roughed up. He was a man about thirty, dressed in a dark business suit, white shirt, and dark tie; he had a thin face with a small precise mustache, and a long nose and very bushy eyebrows. There was a dark bruise on one cheekbone, and his mouth was cut: he dabbed at it gently.

"It didn't seem to be any use arguing with these—er—My name is James Jordan, I just got into town this morning and I was trying to find this address where there's a room advertised for rent."

"Ooh, the liar!" said the woman. "Thank God you caught him—I knew right off, Geraldine just terrified, run in and said a strange man—"

"I asked the little girl about the address—she was the only person on the street, and I—"

"*That's* a story, all right," growled the older man.

"Er—you'll find the stub of my bus ticket in my jacket pocket," said Jordan, not moving. "I just got in from Chicago. I don't know what the hell this is all about, but I do know that the L.A. police are O.K., so when I heard—er—Wild Bill Hickok there phoning the cops, I just sat tight till you got here." He dabbed at his mouth. "I work for Hooper Falls —bond papers, typewriter ribbons, mimeograph supplies, all stationery items—I just got transferred out here, and I wanted a room while I looked around. That's all I asked the little girl about, the street must take a jog or something. And the next thing I knew she went off like a bomb and the whole neighborhood came out and fell on me."

"Likely—"

Hackett stepped forward and felt in the captive's pocket and came up with the stub of a Greyhound bus ticket from Chicago and a check stub for three pieces of baggage at the Greyhound station.

"I've never been known," said Jordan plaintively, "as a guy goes around scaring kids, and you could say I was surprised. But after these two told me seven times over I was a rape-killer I figured I'd just wait for somebody with a little common sense to show up."

Mendoza laughed. "A very smart thing to do. So you're not our boy." He looked at the citizens wryly, cynically, with hidden annoyance. The woman probably a hysterical type. A thin tall woman in pink stretch-pants, a woman with bulging hyperthyroid eyes and an incipient goiter, still panting and gabbling. The two straightforward good citizens who had bravely run to capture an enemy of society. "Mrs.—?"

"Pike, I'm Mrs. Pike, and Geraldine was terrified and I just knew—I've warned her—"

"Just exactly what did Geraldine—your daughter?—say? Where is she? Did she—?"

"She's at home, of course. Safe at home next door. I told her to—Well, I don't remember what she said, but she was terrified, and she said a strange man—and I looked and he was just walking down the street—"

"Went off like a bomb," said Jordan, dabbing at his mouth. "I stopped and asked her if the street went on past the jog at the corner, and she just went off. Screaming at the top of her voice. Ordinary-looking kid, I thought maybe she was retarded, extra shy or something. Now—"

"*You thought—!*" Mrs. Pike was temporarily struck dumb with fury. She choked. "*My Geraldine—*"

"Calm down, calm down," said Mendoza. "Just a little mistake, Mr. Jordan. Mmh—halfway understandable."

The older man let go of Jordan reluctantly. "You mean he *ain't?* That one? We sure thought—be damned, if he ain't, I guess we got off on the wrong foot, but Mis' Pike was yellin' out he tried to rape the little girl, and that other one bein' around this area, we—"

Jordan stood up and smoothed his dark hair. "You've had a murder around here? Sorry to disappoint you, but I'm not X. Quite an introduction to your fair city."

"Apologies, Mr. Jordan," said Mendoza. "I hope you won't feel like suing the—mmh—overenthusiastic citizens."

"Sue!" said Mrs. Pike.

"Oh, now, look," said Herkimer nervously, "all we did—I'm sure sorry, mister, but how could we know—Mis' Pike yellin' and all—"

"Not much harm done," said Jordan, "and quite a story to tell." He squinted down at the darkening bruise on his cheek. "But on second thoughts, I believe I'll get a cab and check into a hotel uptown. . . ."

"And we can guess," said Mendoza, switching on the ignition, "how that damn-fool female has *warned* little Geraldine so thoroughly she's terrified of any stranger. Where's the line between common sense and deliberately scaring the kids?"

"Maybe it depends on the kids," said Hackett thoughtfully; and Higgins looked at him.

"You may have something there, Art."

The ballistics report was in on the gun the young punks had used. It was a .32 revolver, no definite make, could have been an S. and W. .32 long or a Colt .32, one of several models.

The warrant on Bessinger and the McFarleys had come through. Palliser hadn't come back, and Piggott was typing a report on the suicide. Grace was still busy on the Wheeler thing. Inquest on Marla tomorrow: on Blodgett probably on Monday.

Mendoza yawned. "I'll serve the warrant on Bessinger. Tom said another date set up tonight. *Ora esta, ora esotro*. I wonder what'll turn up tomorrow. . . ." And there were still a lot of the known perverts, the possibles, to locate and lean on.

He drove home to Rayo Grande Avenue in Hollywood. And he couldn't shelve, out of hours, all the misery and blood and grief and tragedy; but he had to try to push it aside a little, make room for his own life. As he got out of the car he muttered to himself, "The fools following their natural bent— *como sí*—Kipling always has the word for it."

He started for the back door. That dog was still there, tied to the railing. Nobody had answered the ad. The idiot lost dog. The dog, he thought, looked rather forlorn and lonesome there. He swerved course and said amiably, "So nobody's claimed you, *bufón?*"

Cedric rose pleasedly and grinned at him, offered a paw, tossed the face veil of shaggy hair to show his wall-eye. "The sycophant," said Mendoza. He roughed the hairy head. "So long as you don't upset my cats." And he'd said, an idiot to get lost, but now it occurred to him that there were the irresponsible people, the damnable, careless, uncaring people who did go off and abandon animals. A long while back, he remembered, he'd signed that petition that eventually had made it the law in this state—a misdemeanor carrying a fifty-buck fine. Too little. For the kitten grown to a cat too much trouble to feed, for the amusing puppy unwanted as a dog—

Nobody answering the ad for Cedric. "Did they go away and leave you, *bufón?*" Cedric whimpered. Mendoza pulled his ears and went on in the back door.

"I see nobody's answered the ad, *amante.*"

"I can't understand it," said Alison. "A purebred dog, you'd think—You're early, dinner in twenty minutes. And, Luis, the funniest thing—you should have *seen* Bast."

"*¿Cómo?* What's she up to now?"

"Well, the others have just given Cedric a wide berth mostly, and pretended he isn't there, though Nefertite did steal his hamburger this noon—but Bast spent the whole day, nearly, just curled up *looking* at him. Just out of range of his tongue. As if she was trying to hypnotize him or something. Poor Cedric nearly went frantic trying to lick her—it *is* funny how he seems to like cats—and then the twins distracted him, they're mad about him and when anybody does claim him—*ay de mí*, I don't look forward to it! And when I say the others ignore him, well, Sheba hisses at him whenever she goes past—but Bast *was* funny."

"Poor Cedric," said Mendoza. "I'm going out again tonight. But not, I think, for long." That Bessinger. Talk about fools.

Chapter Six

"THIS Bessinger I still don't believe," said Galeano as they got out of the Ferrari. The police wagon drew up behind to wait silently. "They're all pretty stupid, but I never ran across one quite *so* stupid as that. All I can figure is"—they were walking up to the duplex on Malabar Avenue—"he must figure everybody in the world is as stupid as he is. Or as no good."

"Even stupider than that, Nick," said Mendoza. "He's either too scared or too cautious to do his own murder, so he walks up to the first able-bodied man he sees when the notion occurs to him." He put his finger on the bell.

After a minute the door opened cautiously. "That you?"

"It is us," said Mendoza, and shoved the door wide and went in. Galeano had his gun out, just in case. "Mr. William Bessinger, I presume. May we have some lights, please?" Galeano found the switch.

"Is that them, Bill?" The blonde in purple pyjamas appeared in the doorway to the right.

"In," said Mendoza, and Galeano gestured with the gun.

"Hey, what is this?" asked Bessinger weakly. "What—?" He backed from the tiny entrance hall into the living room, the blonde retreating behind him. Another man was there, a stout youngish man drinking beer.

"Mr. and Mrs. Ronald McFarley. Lieutenant Mendoza, L.A.P.D. I have here a warrant to arrest all three of you on a charge of conspiring to commit homicide in the first degree. I am—"

"*What?*" yelped the blonde. "I didn't have nothing to—"

"*Homicide?*" said Bessinger. "We ain't done no murder—"

"Now see what you got me into, damn it," said McFarley. "I said you were crazy—"

"But we ain't *done* nothing!" wailed Bessinger. "Nothing at all—oh, damn them two loudmouths, why'd they hafta go talking? Why—?"

"One of them is a police officer," said Mendoza. "We're taking you in now. Come on. You can call your lawyer from jail."

"*Fuzz?*" said Bessinger in naked astonishment. "I don't get any of this. I thought I could smell fuzz—and we ain't done a single damn thing, and you say homicide—it just ain't fair!"

They all went on saying that in various ways all the way down to the new facility on Alameda. Galeano at least found it entertaining.

"Comment on the average amoral I.Q.," grunted Mendoza. "I don't think it's so damn funny, Nick."

"Not funny exactly," said Galeano. "Encouraging. Reassuring. For those of us who have to cope with them. Even the dumbest cop on the most backward force in the country—and there really aren't so many of those any more—knows better than to do a fool thing like that."

"*Vaya,* you've got a point," admitted Mendoza, and went home. Alison was also highly amused at the bumbling Bessinger.

"You wouldn't believe it in a detective novel, would you? Oh, well, if you're going to have a drink, some of that peppermint liqueur, please. But it *is* funny, Luis. What will they get?"

"Bessinger'll get a stiff one on the armed robbery, plus this. Could be life. The McFarley's, probably a one-to-three." Mendoza went out to the kitchen, to be confronted by the back views of three cats all sitting absolutely silent on the deep windowsill overlooking the backyard: in the middle, the broad black rear of El Señor, his blond-in-reverse Siamese markings invisible from behind; on either side, the diminutive brown backs of Sheba and Nefertite. Intent, they stared out the window into the dark where the strange monster reposed, tied to the railing.

Mendoza burst into laughter, and as one cat they turned and gave him a cold-eyed stare.

"*Perdón*," he said meekly, and got down the bottle of rye. El Señor's one vice overcame his curiosity; he abandoned the vigil and demanded his share in a raucous voice. Mendoza gave him half an ounce in a saucer, poured Alison's liqueur, and went back to the living room, a shot glass in either hand.

"Nothing more in on that poor child?" she asked, sipping.

"*Nada*. Tomorrow is also a day. Something may show. I hope."

Thursday turned out to be a day they got out and around. It was Hackett's day off. Still a lot of the known perverts out of Records to find, and Higgins and Piggott were just about to take off on the legwork—Palliser had got together with Jason Grace over Goldberg's notes on the punks—when Sergeant Lake relayed an outside call.

"Mendoza, Homicide."

"My name's Montmorency," said a forthright voice. "You won't know me, Lieutenant, and could be I'm out of line—who am I to tell the L.A.P.D. its business—but I thought I'd call. I'm a P.A. officer here."

"Oh. Oh?"

"And could be he came right to your mind, for all I know you've got him there for questioning right now. I just thought in case you hadn't—because between you and me I thought the board was crazy to let him out. Even after fifteen years."

"Who?" asked Mendoza interestedly.

"Ackerman. Edward Ackerman. It doesn't ring a bell? Well, he wouldn't be in your files. Pasedena's. Rape-murder of an eleven-year-old, sixteen years back. After the usual prior record. A pretty messy murder. He's six months out, and I'm his P.A. officer. I don't much like him."

"Now you don't say," said Mendoza gently. "I do."

Montmorency laughed unhappily. "I just thought—well, he ought to be looked at, Lieutenant. On this poor Pickens kid.

I'll send over his file, shall I? He's living in Hollywood, got a job as a janitor over at a little office building on Santa Monica, and a room at a private house." He added both addresses. "I wondered—even if you knew his name, you might not have known he was out of Quentin."

"Neither. But he sounds very interesting," said Mendoza. *"Muchas gracias."*

"I just thought—well, I'll send over his file."

"He just thought—" Mendoza laughed, relaying that, "Suppose you go see if you can find him. He could be very hot for it."

"On P.A. he's not supposed to be driving, and without a car he couldn't have—" began Higgins.

"Not supposed to is the operative phrase. Go look for him," said Mendoza.

Higgins and Piggott went out, and half an hour later brought him in; he'd been on his job at the office building. By then, Montmorency had sent his file down by private messenger, and Mendoza was thinking that Ackerman looked very hot indeed. He was annoyed; if Montmorency hadn't thought twice and called in, they wouldn't know a damned thing about Ackerman.

The expected pedigree. Exposure, solicitation of minors, attempted rape. What had put him away for fifteen years was the murder: and it could be a model for Marla's murder. The little girl snatched off the street, only in this case that had been witnessed: raped and murdered up by the Eaton Canyon reservoir, beaten and strangled. He'd been traced by the description of his pickup truck, had never confessed but been convicted on plenty of laboratory evidence. Mendoza wondered what his blood type was. That scrap of cloth in Marla's mouth—

He looked at Ackerman coldly when they brought him in. The man even looked the part, which they didn't always: a shabby, rather dirty middle-aged man, not very big but with furtive eyes and a thin-lipped mouth and an awkward shuffling gait.

They started to question him. Where were you last Thursday morning, a week ago today?—down near Echo Park?—what about the little girl, Ackerman, Marla?—did you see her, did you pick her up?—so, you were at your job, can you prove it? —did anyone see you there?

It was uphill work. He'd had a lot of dealing with cops, and he knew the value of silence. He said as little as possible, and that reluctantly. He didn't even swear at them and call them dirty names; he just glowered at them under his brows. He didn't do that, he was at the job, he was clean, he didn't have no car, he didn't know what they were talking about.

After a while Higgins and Piggott went out to try to check his alibi, while Mendoza and Glasser went on at him. "Say," said Piggott as they passed the desk, "where's Tom Landers? I haven't seen him this morning."

"He went out on—" began Sergeant Lake, and the phone rang and he picked it up.

"Always something," said Piggott. "Want to take my car or yours?"

They took Higgins'. And that errand left them up in the air, because while it was all suggestive, it didn't give them anything solid, really.

They found the manager of the building where Ackerman worked. Who said uneasily, "Has he *done* something? Sure, I know he's an ex-con, I took the gamble. . . . Last Thursday morning? Hell, I couldn't swear he was here before ten o'clock, when I got here. Then, he was here. No, the tenants wouldn't see him ordinarily, but you can ask." They asked. Nobody had seen Ackerman prior to ten o'clock or so; only the manager had seen him then. And of course that said nothing; he could have done the murder and been there by ten. Or he could have been there all the time.

They went to where he had a room, on Barton Avenue, and that was also suggestive and also nothing solid. The landlady was a dim-witted trusting soul who rented out four rooms in a big house. She had been away all last Thursday, from eight in the morning on, "with a lady friend down to the beach," and she had an old Ford, and she'd left the keys at home, she wasn't sure exactly where.

It was up in the air.

"*¡Mil rayos!*" said Mendoza when he heard all that. "But it *is* suggestive. I like him for it, boys. Damn it, I wonder if we could get a warrant to look at that car—look at his room, his clothes—it's nothing concrete, but put it all together—damn it, we'll try. We can hold him twenty-four hours without a charge."

"You won't get a warrant just on that," said Piggott pessimistically.

"We can try. Take him down to jail." Mendoza got on the phone to the courthouse.

By the time they got back from seeing a sullen Ackerman into a cell, it was twelve-thirty and they were all ready for lunch. They were just leaving for Federico's when Lake, seeing Mendoza march past, beckoned and held out the phone.

"What *now?*" said Mendoza.

"Homicide? This is the Traffic garage, sir. We got a routine call to tow in an abandoned car this morning, and it was brought in about an hour ago. One of the men just happened to notice a—er—peculiar odor, and, well, there seems to be a body in the trunk, sir. A male body. We just—er—looked and found it."

"*¡Porvida! ¿Y después? ¡Eso ya es llover sobre mojado!*" said Mendoza loudly. "My God, everything happens to us! I will be damned. I will be—All right, we'll be down to look. After lunch. Don't touch it."

"Oh, no, sir. We just thought—"

"You ought to call. Thanks so much." Mendoza hung up and passed that one on.

"Oh, for God's sake," said Higgins. "As if we hadn't enough to do." Piggott just shut his eyes and looked resigned.

"Lunch," said Mendoza. "The body will keep. By the way, Jimmy, where's Tom? I haven't laid eyes on him today."

"He went out—as a matter of fact, I'm surprised he hasn't called in," said Lake, "on—" the phone shrilled and he picked it up. Mendoza waved a dismissing hand and went on out.

Palliser and Grace had spent an abortive morning asking questions of principals and teachers at all the schools, repeating the descriptions they had of the three young punks. Within the fairly wide area in which the holdups had occurred, there were five junior high schools and three high schools possible as harboring the punks; and the descriptions were rather definite; but everybody they talked to dutifully thought and said, no, they couldn't place any of those kids at all.

At noon they knocked off and discussed it gloomily over sandwiches at a drugstore. "I can't figure it, Jase," said Palliser. "That age, they must be in school if they're not dropouts, and even if they were it'd be fairly recent, some one of the principals would remember them even now."

"If they were running together before they dropped out," said Grace, eyeing his chocolate malt. "Maybe they came up from Santa Monica."

"Maybe they came over from Glendale," said Palliser. "Outside this area, anyway. Try schools farther away?"

"I'm out of ideas. That's the indicated direction," said Grace. "One thing I will say, you just never do know what the young punks are going to do. They don't know themselves."

"On that I'll have to agree," said Palliser. "All right, we cast farther afield. At least it's nice weather."

They went down to the Traffic garage at one o'clock to see the new body. The car was an old Pontiac sedan. Scarne and Duke met them there, and Dr. Bainbridge came bustling in after them.

The body in the trunk was that of a young man about thirty, and he had been shot in the head. "About two days dead, at a guess," said Bainbridge. He lifted the body gently and Scarne began emptying the pockets of the plain dark business suit. The first thing they came up with was an empty billfold that still carried the I.D. if no cash. Martin Sutcliffe, an address in Fresno.

"So," said Mendoza to the garage attendant, "where did the car come from?"

"It was reported this morning, sir. Citizen called in and said it had been in front of his house since Tuesday night and he'd just looked and it hadn't any registration in it, so would we come get it. We sent a tow truck. It was just down from Sunset on Las Dimas in Hollywood."

"Oh. Well, you go over the car and see what turns up," said Mendoza to Scarne. "Let's see if anybody in Fresno knows Sutcliffe." They went back to the office and he told Lake to get him the police department in Fresno. "Adding insult to injury, my God, with this rapist running loose and—Lieutenant Mendoza, Homicide, L.A.P.D. Have you by any chance lost a Mr. Martin Sutcliffe of one-four-nine Del Paso Way in your fair city?"

"Sergeant Curtis. *Sutcliffe?* We have indeed. Don't tell me— did you say *homicide?*"

"Yes. He's just turned up here dead. Shot. In the back of an old Pontiac." Sergeant Lake would be relaying the plate number up to the D.M.V. in Sacramento. "What have you got on him?"

"Oh, my God!" said Curtis. "That poor young guy. What happened to him? Nice quiet respectable fellow—my God, he sold me a car a couple of months ago—salesman at a Ford agency here. He wasn't married, he lived with his sister, Anita Sutcliffe—she reported him missing on Tuesday. He went out to a movie on Monday night and never came home. We found his car not far away from the theater, we couldn't figure—not the type to go on a tear, and—my God, *shot?*"

"Yes, well, we'll need a formal identification. From somebody. We'll let you know what turns up, Sergeant."

"Yes," said Curtis automatically. "My God, murdered—and somebody'll have to tell the sister—thanks for letting us know. But I can't figure—he wasn't the type to—What? Yes, we asked her that, he'd have had about forty dollars on him, she thought."

"Price of a life?" said Mendoza, putting the phone down. Well, he had known murder done for less. And more. And for nothing at all.

A couple of bums had got fighting with bottles over on the Row and one of them had got his head cracked open. Glasser was out on that. Sergeant Lake was too busy to take up his crossword puzzle. The Lieutenant asked him to get the Wilcox Street precinct, a Sergeant Barth—"Be invading his territory, after all"—and then Jason Grace called to check in, see if anything urgent had come up, his deep soft voice warm in Lake's ear even when he was only saying, "We're feeling kind of stymied—nothing showing at all."

"Well, we've had this and that, but I don't guess urgent enough for you to stop the legwork," said Lake.

"I was afraid you'd say that, Jimmy." Grace chuckled and hung up.

Sergeant Lake was beginning to be just slightly worried about Tom Landers. Tom was conscientious as a rule, and it had been only a couple of minutes past eight when he'd taken off after that guy, and here it was two-forty and no word from him at all. Which wasn't like Tom.

When Mendoza came out of his office, with Higgins and Piggott after him, all looking preoccupied, Lake said, "Say, Lieutenant—about—"

"Later, Jimmy." Mendoza went out.

"Say, George, about Tom—"

But Higgins was saying to Piggott, "Look, if the station that landlady goes to could say anything about the mileage on her car, it might give us a handle—if Ackerman did borrow it, and we could show—"

Sergeant Lake was alone in the office. He started to worry a little more. It really wasn't like Tom. And this same fellow had grazed Palliser with a shot only a couple of weeks ago. Suppose—

"Well, of all the funny things," said Sergeant Barth of the Wilcox Street precinct. "But no funnier than a lot we get, all the time. I suppose you want to ask questions around where the car was left. I'll go along—for once, things a little slow here. We get the funny things all right. There was one just lately that really bugged me—still does, as a matter of fact—this—"

"So all right, let's go," said Mendoza. *Dios,* with everything

else, and the rapist loose—Ackerman? He looked so very hot
for it, but all the red tape—that warrant—

"All right," said Barth amiably.

Landers had had an extremely frustrating day. He had arrived at the office at a few minutes after eight, late, and just
as he had been about to join the others in Mendoza's office,
Lake had had a call. One of their informants, saying that if
they still wanted that Jeff Gadsworthy, he was having breakfast at a drugstore on Pico Boulevard.

Gadsworthy, who had got away from Palliser a couple of
weeks back, had escaped from the state pen in Maryland and
was urgently wanted; he was to be considered dangerous. "I'll
see if I can nab him," said Landers. "You tell the Lieutenant."
Which Lake had not been able to do.

Landers' Corvair was stubborn about starting; he cussed it.
Needed a new battery, probably. But he got it going finally,
went out Pico, and parked around the corner from that drugstore. He had just started down there, when ten steps from
the door he spotted Gadsworthy coming out. Gadsworthy, all
right—there'd been a flyer on him now, with a mug shot—
Landers broke into a lope, but Gadsworthy had too big a
start; two minutes later Landers, running hard, watched him
take off down Pico in a sky-blue Ford sedan. Just a chance
—He ran back for the Corvair, and muttering desperately,
"Come *on,* girl, come *on,*" got it to start right off. He went
down Pico recklessly, cussing at the signals, and where San
Vicente crossed he spotted the sky-blue Ford in the block
ahead.

After that, frustration was piled on frustration. He kept
looking for a squad car, his attention triply divided among
the Ford, driving in traffic, and keeping a lookout for the welcome black-and-white sedan with the roof-mounted light. He
saw some, oh, yes, and little use they were to him. One waiting for a light on a cross street, the Ford half a block ahead
then, traffic thick, and by the time he saw it he was past the
intersection: a minute's delay would mean losing Gadsworthy.
By the time he had hung on as far down Venice Boulevard as

Lincoln, Landers was thinking that every police-officer's private car should be equipped with police radio. He had seen at least a dozen police cars, L.A.P.D., Beverly Hills, Highway Patrol, and it had been impossible to signal any of them. Several had passed him going in the opposite direction. All he was concentrated on now was hanging onto the Ford.

Where the hell was Gadsworthy going? He turned down Ocean Park Boulevard to hit the coast highway, Landers three cars behind. A couple of blocks down Ocean Park, Landers had spotted a Santa Monica squad car in the right lane going the same way, and taking a chance, had leaned over awkwardly to roll down the right-hand window and direct a quick shout as he passed—"L.A.P.D.—wanted man ahead, take him!" But in all the traffic noise, only his voice had carried, and the driver turned an angry look, evidently thinking one of the cop-baiting citizens was jeering, and whisked the squad car around the next corner.

Afterward, Landers thought if he'd taken the chance, stopped in traffic, and hailed a squad car definitely—but he hadn't a notion where Gadsworthy was heading, in town the Ford could be lost in minutes, and as matters stood he was at least *on* him.

At any rate, he didn't stop. He stayed grimly on the Ford's tail, two and three cars behind, up the Malibu Highway, past Malibu, past Amarillo Beach, past Solstice Beach, past Escondido Beach—where the *hell* was Gadsworthy going? In all those miles never a police car passed in either direction. There was the usual amount of heavy-enough traffic, even beyond the metropolis—this was the much-traveled coast highway to all points north—and he didn't think an inconspicuous white Corvair would be spotted as a tail. But he was beginning to be very glad he'd started with a full tank of gas this morning.

Now if the Ford had to stop for gas—Landers prayed it would. He hung on past Encinal Beach, and on and on. The Ford kept to a steady fifty in the middle lane. Landers debated trying to crowd him over, into the shoulder—if he'd been in the right lane, he might have taken the chance, but as it was with steady traffic in all lanes—you had to think of the citizens.

Gadsworthy wasn't driving fast, plenty of traffic passing in the left lane, but he was making steady time. Landers couldn't take the chance.

The Ford entered the outskirts of Oxnard at ten-forty-five. What if he had to slow down in town?—but he didn't have to. The highway just skirted the town, and the Ford kept to the highway. No police car in sight. But damn it, he'd have to stop sometime to fill the tank—

They pulled into Ventura at eleven-twenty. The Ford turned off into the town. Not a village exactly, but a lot smaller than L.A., and when Landers spotted a black-and-white police car he slammed on the brakes, jumped out, and waved it down.

"L.A.P.D.," he said urgently to the driver. "Quick—blue Ford up ahead, plate number FQL–700—a wanted man, escapee— probably armed—get on him, for God's—"

The driver was quick; it didn't need the badge in Landers' hand to convince him. He gunned the car; Landers leaped back into the Corvair. Two blocks up he came on the squad car, the halted Ford, and two uniformed men just slapping the cuffs on Gadsworthy.

"I hope this isn't a practical joke," said the driver. He eyed Landers' badge, and the gun his partner had just found in the Ford. "Not a practical joke. Who is he?"

Landers told them. "I'd better take him back with me."

"You're in Ventura County. A little red tape before we release him to the L.A.P.D.," said the other man dryly. "You look a bit beat."

"I've been on the damned guy since eight-thirty," said Landers.

"Be damned. Well, we've got a jail. We'll take him in while the red tape gets wound up, and I guess you could stand a cup of coffee. My name's O'Reilly. That's Farbstein."

"Landers. I could do with that. And I suppose I'd better report in, everybody'll be wondering where I am."

Gadsworthy looked dispiritedly down at the cuffs and said nothing at all. They put him in the squad car and drove to the Ventura police station, and Landers, offered a phone, asked for L.A.P.D. Central Headquarters.

"I'm sorry, sir, our out-of-city lines are temporarily out of order," sang the operator.

"Oh, hell," said Landers.

"I understand," said Farbstein, "that some vital power line got knocked out by an amorous Angus bull that got loose. Here's your coffee. Cream, sugar?"

"Come to the country and see life," said Landers. "And all to oblige Maryland. What the hell do I care about Maryland's crime statistics? *Or* escapees? Thanks very much."

Outside phone service wasn't restored by two-forty-five when the red tape was wound up and he could take Gadsworthy back. The Ventura fellows had been very nice, bought him lunch and asked a lot of questions about how that top force down there operated; but he should have reported in.

He went to get the Corvair, bring it round to the entrance and load Gadsworthy, still cuffed, into it, and found the battery dead. But very dead. The engine wouldn't even try to turn over.

"Jesus H. Christ!" said Landers, who was normally the mildest and most non-profane of men. "And"—ungratefully—"in this one-horse burg, where can I get it even recharged enough to—"

In the end, they flagged a Highway Patrol car to ferry Gadsworthy down to L.A., and Landers wasn't able to get a phone call through until 4 P.M.

"You know something I just thought of?" said Palliser. "By God, Jase!"

"You've had an idea?" They were just coming out of the twelfth school in which they'd been asking about the young punks.

"Maybe I have. Look, on all these jobs, by Goldberg's notes, it just suddenly occurred to me, the times are roughly the same. Noon. Twelve-fifteen. Just after noon. Twelve-forty-five. About noon." Palliser riffled through the notes. "Lunch hour. No?"

"Um," said Grace. "Yes indeedy."

"*School* lunch hour. Isn't it? Mostly? Twelve to one?"

"Yes," said Grace thoughtfully, "but—"

"But that says whatever school it is, it couldn't be very far off where all these jobs were done. They couldn't have come up from Avalon or anywhere. Why haven't they showed at some school?"

"Dropouts," said Grace.

"And the times just a coincidence? It seems funny, that's all," said Palliser.

Bast was still watching the stranger, closely and acutely. Most certainly he did not behave like Dog. She was still uncertain about him.

"But, *Mamacíta,* Sheba 'n' Nefertite inside—'n' Bast 'n' El Señor—"

"He doesn't belong to us like the cats, Terry," said Alison. "Somebody else owns—well, belongs to him—you mustn't—"

"But, *Mama*—"

Nobody at all had called about the ad. Found, English sheepdog, tag on collar *Cedric,* vicinity Hollywood Boulevard and Yucca.

Chapter Seven

THE CITIZEN who had called about the abandoned Pontiac lived three houses down Las Dimas from Sunset. His name was William Blake.

"*Blake?*" said Barth.

"Why not?" said Blake. "It's a perfeckly good name, isn't it? And what's with this, did I notice who left that car there? What the hell does it matter who left it? It was left. Nor I don't figure I got a monopoly on the street, mister, a guy parks in front of my house an hour, two hours, O.K.—but I got a car and my son's got a car and there's only a one-car garage, and if the other one goes in the driveway one of us is all the time havin' to back out for the other one. You get me. So when that car's in front since Tuesday night, and I look and see there ain't no registration in it—"

"So you didn't see whoever left it. Thanks very—" began Barth.

"The stupid things people do I don't try to explain," said Blake, shrugging his narrow shoulders. "A theory I got, I tell you. Everybody so damned scared of this fallout. You ask me, I got a theory that it's already fell. About twenty years back, I figure. Only what it did, it didn't kill people or start plagues, it just dried up most of the common sense in people's heads. You look around, see what's goin' on, how people act, maybe you think it's a kind of plausible idea. Sorry I can't help you, mister."

"And I've heard less plausible," said Mendoza. "He may have something there."

This was worth an hour of time, no more. It could be that someone had seen whoever had parked the Pontiac. It wasn't very probable. This little street off Sunset was middle-class residential, a couple of apartments farther down the block, mostly single houses. Mendoza and Barth hadn't found anyone at home at the first two houses; the one next to Blake's was empty also; but at the next house they hit an unexpected jackpot. Her name was Mehitabel Twelvetrees; she was about sixty and she was fat, suspiciously black-haired, rosy-cheeked, and wherever her Maker had set her down she would have known everything there was to know about her neighbors and surroundings.

She said promptly, to Mendoza's question, "Yessir, I did. It wasn't any of my business, I didn't bother to tell Mr. Blake, what did it matter, he called and the police come for it, and they never asked me so I figure it wasn't important. Now you come asking and so I tell you I did. See who parked that car."

"You did?" said Barth. It was such a long chance.

"Yessir, I did. I was waiting on my husband—he was late, had some overtime work. It was a nice mild night, I was setting out on the porch. No need for the porch light, I was just setting. Warm for February, we generally do get two, three warm days, but it's due to change back any time, I dare say."

"Well, who did?" asked Mendoza. "Did you get any kind of look at him?"

"Them. 'Twas a man and woman. Roundabout eight o'clock Tuesday night. There's a streetlight there by Mr. Blake's drive. They come pushin' the old car, or rather him, she was steering it, up the street—I guess it'd died and they couldn't get it started. She steered it into the curb there and got out, and they stood and argued quite a spell. I couldn't hear much, except the man sayin', 'Oh, honey,' and I guess she was mad. Finally they got a couple of suitcases out of the back seat and started up the street. *And* I can tell you where they went," said Mrs. Twelvetrees. "You see that there motel up on the corner? The Sunshine Motel. They went up there and I see them turn in the parking lot. Prob'ly they figured to stay there till they got the car fixed, but nobody come after it until Mr. Blake called the police."

Mendoza and Barth looked at each other incredulously. It wasn't, of course, possible that the quarry was still there; it wasn't even probable that she was right. "Are you sure of that, ma'am?" asked Barth. "Well, why on—why didn't you tell Blake when he complained about the car? These people—"

She drew herself up. "Of course I'm sure. Wouldn't say so if I wasn't. And he never complained to *me*. You come asking polite, I tell you what I know, *which* is all a body can do."

"Oh, yes. We can go and ask," said Barth to Mendoza doubtfully.

"I don't believe it," said Mendoza.

"Oh, neither do I. But—"

They went up there and found the motel manager. "A couple registering on Tuesday night with baggage but no car? You're *police?* Well, *at* that I nearly called you last night. I did indeed. And what's more, they're still here. A Mr. and Mrs. Carl Nugent."

"Oh, I don't believe it at all," said Mendoza. There was a catch in it some place. Nobody could be so stupid as to—

"Twelve-A," said the manager. "They've been there all the time since, far as I know. And last night there was quite a lot of noise—the tenants on either side complaining. You *want* them for something? Well, this is a respectable place, but you never do know about people. I'm only too glad to cooperate."

He bustled ahead of them with a passkey, opened the door, and stood aside. Mendoza and Barth went in.

Twelve-A was, or had been, a pleasantly furnished, ordinary motel room: twin beds, bath off to the left, a walk-in closet, television in one corner, a table, an upholstered chair, plain beige carpet. Now it was in the wildest confusion. Bedspreads and blankets tangled together on the floor, two suitcases strewed their contents on top of them, a dirty pink chiffon negligee hung on the chair, an empty fifth of Johnny Walker stood on top of the television, and two bottles of vodka lay just inside the door, one empty, the other trickling its remaining contents onto the rug. A pile of male clothing was heaped in the middle of the room, and a pair of spike-heeled, patent-leather shoes lay nearby. A man lay on the bed farthest from the door, and from the bathroom came faint splashings. The man was naked except for a pair of cotton shorts, and he had a wet towel wrapped around his head. He turned slowly on one side and managed to open one eye to peer at the invaders.

"Who're you?"

"Carl? Carl! You still alive?" The woman appeared in the bathroom door, wiping her face with a towel. She was a well-stacked blonde-by-request, simply clad in pink panties and pink brassiere. "And just who the hell are you?" she added, startled, staring at Mendoza and Barth and the manager.

"Mrs. Nugent?" said Mendoza. "This is Mr. Nugent?" The man just groaned.

"So what?"

"Did you leave a Pontiac sedan parked down Las Dimas on Tuesday night before you registered here?"

"Oh, for God's sake," said the blonde disgustedly, "I suppose there's a law or something, twenty-four-hour parking. We was going to call a garage, but Carl kept putting it off. There's a fine or something—Carl! Hey, lover-man, it's about the car—your car." She stared at Mendoza again. "But hey, what the hell, a plainclothes man-hunter come with a parking ticket? Big deal. Hey, Carl! It's about your *car.*"

"Mr. Nugent," said Mendoza, and stepped to the bed and hauled him upright. "Is the Pontiac your car? The D.M.V. will tell us, if you don't. The Pontiac you left down the street there?"

Nugent groaned and opened his eyes. "I got a hell of a hang-over," he complained. "You're fuzz. About—the Pontiac. My car—" Comprehension was dawning in his bloodshot eyes, and he groaned again, more feelingly. "Oh, my God," he said. "Oh, my God. I don't never have no kind of luck at all."

"It's just a parking ticket," said the blonde. She put on the chiffon negligee, in no hurry. "Big deal."

"Oh, my God," said Nugent.

"The Pontiac," said Mendoza, "with the body in the trunk, Mr. Nugent. Would you care to explain the body?"

"All my life, I never had a thing but the bad breaks," mourned Nugent, clutching his head.

"A *body?*" said the blonde blankly.

"The body of Martin Sutcliffe of Fresno. Dead since Monday night, probably."

"A b——" Suddenly the blonde went off like a siren. She stood there and screamed, the negligee hanging open. Barth went over and slapped her hard, and a scream cut off in mid-air and she collapsed into the chair.

"Oh, was that his name?" said Nugent. "Listen, it was an accident. The gun went off. I never meant to kill the guy."

"You mean to *tell* me I been riding around with a *dead body* in that car? Oh, Christ," said the blonde. "Oh, my God. You *killed* a guy, and you let me—oh, my God, I need a drink —I think there's still some vodka—" She groped into the bathroom.

"Listen, this is all wrong, we haven't warned him," said Barth. "You know damn well the court'll throw it out if he confesses before we've—"

"Oh, hell," said Mendoza, and repeated the set piece. All the rights, and did Nugent want a lawyer, and he needn't say anything. Nugent just moaned and shook his head. The blonde came back with a shot glass in one shaky hand, and spilled a little as she drank.

"Mrs. Nugent, were you aware—?"

"For God's sake, don't call me that! I never laid *eyes* on him till Tuesday. Last Tuesday. My God. A body. Let it be a lesson to little Louella, don't take up with strangers." She sat down again and swallowed vodka, shuddering. "I just needed a ride down from Fresno to the big town, he seemed like a nice guy and all, and I mean, fair exchange, don't get me wrong, I'm not a pro—he had all this liquor in the car, and I been down on my luck, no objections to making a night of it—but if I'd *known*—You *killed* a guy?" She stared at Nugent.

He sat up in bed looking miserable, a paunchy dark man

about forty, with a round immature face and thinning hair. "Oh, gee, everything always goes wrong for me. I mighta known. I mighta *known*. If I'd just left him there—but I had to get smart. People seen me talkin' to him in that bar. After the movie—we just happened to go into the bar at the same time. I thought, take and dump him in the ocean down here. Or something. I wouldn't've held him up atall, but I seen him pay for his drink, he only had one, and it looked like a good roll, only it turned out it was only forty-two bucks—I got the lousiest luck of any guy in the world—and the gun going off and all. I never meant to *kill* the guy, but there I was—stuck." He looked at them unhappily, pathetically.

Mendoza still didn't believe it. Things never got quite so simple as this. Except, of course, sometimes when they did. "All right, both of you get dressed," he said. "We're taking you in."

"Not *me!*" wailed the blonde. "Say, I don't know one damn thing about this—he picked me up in Fresno on Tuesday, I'd never laid eyes on him before, and if I'd known he had a body in the trunk, for God's sake, I'd—well, I tell you, it's a lesson to me, Louella Norman don't pick up any more strangers! My God, you can't arrest me, I hadn't a damn thing to do with—"

"There may not be a charge, but you're coming in now to make a statement at least," said Mendoza. "Get dressed."

Sometimes it got just this simple. And it was gratifying, of course, to get one cleared up so fast.

They took the pair downtown and Barth said regretfully he'd better get back to his own beat. "We do run into the funny ones. Now and then. Nice to've seen you again, Mendoza."

While Glasser took down the blonde's statement—they'd booked Nugent straight in, pending the warrant—Lake told Mendoza about Landers and his frustrating day. "He's still stuck up there, but the Highway Patrol delivered Gadsworthy a while ago. Henry took him to jail and notified the Feds."

"Very gratifying indeed," said Mendoza. And about then Palliser and Grace came in, looking discouraged, and told him about their abortive day. "Now that's damned funny. Considering the ages, *something* should have shown at *some* school about that trio."

"That's what we thought too," said Grace ruefully. "But it didn't. Why not?"

Mendoza rubbed his mustache thoughtfully. "Unless they go to different schools—"

"Then how did they get together?" asked Palliser reasonably.

Scarne came in and said they'd got odds and ends out of that car, and also a gun. In the locked glove compartment. An old Colt .38, with four shells still in it. "Which may help you some."

"*Gracias*. We've already got him," said Mendoza absently.

"What? Well, talk about a Sherlock Holmes. How?"

"Just stupidity," said Mendoza. "Yes, William Blake may have something there—"

"First Kipling, now Blake," said Grace.

"Not that Blake. Yes—mmh—indeed. It's an interesting theory, anyway. Jimmy! Have you heard anything about that search warrant on Ackerman's room?"

"They just called," said Lake, looking in uneasily. "You can't have it."

"*¡Diez millones de demonios! ¡Jesú, José, y Santa María!*" said Mendoza violently. "Why the *hell*—?"

"I told you so," said Piggott, wandering into the office with Higgins in time to hear that.

"Not enough evidence," said Lake.

"Evidence! What the hell more do they—almost the same exact M.O. as on Marla, and we can show he had access to a car—and no alibi—I don't know what the *hell* the damn judges expect—" Mendoza stabbed out his cigarette violently. "He looks like a hot one to me, but if we're not allowed to *look* for any more evidence—"

"So," said Higgins, "do we get him up here and pound at him again, Luis? He's an old hand, he isn't going to break down so easy."

"I *know*, damn it. And, damn it to hell, we can't hold him past tomorrow morning. God damn it, and if he is it, still loose to pick up another Marla—" He lit another cigarette, looking furious.

The inquest on Marla tomorrow. Without much doubt, the open verdict. It just could have been, if they'd got that search warrant, they'd have been able to offer the evidence and get Ackerman—if it had been Ackerman—charged right there. Mendoza said this and that about the court's antecedents, probable personal habits, and inferential motives; but there was nothing he could do about it. He clapped on his hat and went home. It had been quite a day.

Landers got home, with a new battery in the Corvair, at nine o'clock. It was lucky he'd had his checkbook on him. He was tired; it had, all in all, been quite a day. He took a bath, rummaged in the refrigerator and found some cheese, made instant coffee, and got into bed with a recent science-fiction magazine.

He'd been born into the wrong century, that was all. Now with these instant thought-transmitters they had on Mars, he'd just have had to point at one of those squad cars to get the message over, and saved all that running around. Not to speak of the new battery.

Palliser went home to a Roberta poring over house plans in *California Home*. Roberta, however, was a model wife (at least she had been so far) and listened sympathetically to Palliser's account of his unproductive day.

"But how funny, John—if they are all about sixteen, and you had quite good descriptions on the whole—even if they're dropouts they'd have been known in some school at some time fairly—"

"That's if they were running together when they were in school," said Palliser, pacing restlessly up and down the apartment living room. "If they weren't, well, taken separately the descriptions don't amount to much."

"No, I see that."

"And it's just the damn punks like these—getting started early, this bunch—that we like to drop on fast. Maybe make them think twice, the little they have to think with. The kids loose with a gun—the ballistics report was in, it was a .32."

"And where do you suppose they got that?"

"Robin, love, there is no difficulty about acquiring a gun—
not for the punks," said Palliser. "They're trying to make it
harder all the time for the honest citizens who just want to
protect themselves, but any hood who wants a gun can get
one very easy. I'm not worried about the gun—at least I am
only because who knows what innocent market clerk or druggist is going to get shot up next—but I would like, I would
damn well like, to drop on these stupid, lazy, savage little
punks. Who are already out for something for nothing. Aller-
gic to work. Probably already having got into this and that
deviltry—the warning rattle, as the Lieutenant says. Who—"
He stopped dead.

"You've had an inspiration," said Roberta, pleased.

"Insp——my God!" said Palliser. "Why didn't we think of
that?—My God, I'll take a bet—" He swung on her, excited.
"That school—what do they call it, where the kids are sent
who get into trouble at public school. Get expelled, sus-
pended. Corrective, whatever—Jase'll know. I'll bet that's it.
And why neither of us thought of it—"

In late afternoon the mild weather had begun to leave
them; it was still only February. When Mendoza got home the
air was chill and a little wind had risen.

The twins, fetched in two hours ago to have sweaters for-
cibly applied, were now turning the tables with a vengeance.
"Mamá, Cedric all *cold!* you *like* Cedric, *Mamacíta?* Don't
want Cedric—"

"Now look, he's got a nice thick fur coat, Terry."

"Frío out there," said Johnny. *"Pobre* Cedric."

"Oh, my heavens!" said Alison. "You two settle down and
forget it." She pushed Mendoza out of the nursery ahead of
her. Mrs. MacTaggart made soothing noises. The twins looked
at all the unfeeling grown-ups with sorrowful eyes; Terry started
to cry.

"Now, *mo croidhe,* we have our nice warm baths and Máiri'll sing you a song or two to be going to sleep by—would you like 'Bonnie Doon,' or 'We're no' awa' to bide awa'' maybe—"

"*No* bonnie," sobbed Terry. "*Pobrecito* Cedric!"

"That *dog,*" said Alison, sinking into her chair at the table. "That little devil Sheba has discovered he's the world's easiest mark. For cats and children, at least. She ate half the hamburger he was supposed to have for dinner, and Nefertite did the same thing yesterday. He just sat back and watched like a —a doting grandfather. And then, of course, Sheba came in and was sick on the living room carpet. Bast is still trying to hypnotize him. And he looks so *sad* when El Señor hisses at him. The poor boy, he really is a darling, Luis, and he must be missing his people, but he's so good and patient. And wherever he came from—"

"It's very funny that ad hasn't raised somebody. . . . And when I think, *condenación,*" said Mendoza, attacking his veal chop as if it were an enemy, "of that damned judge—Ackerman could very well be the boy we want, but when we're not allowed to—"

"Yes, very annoying," said Alison. "One like that. The little girls. I don't suppose, Luis, the judge has any little girls, or ever had, because if so he might have stretched a point. . . . That wind *has* got up." She poured coffee and passed it over.

Mendoza drank a quarter of a cup at one swallow. "I could say this and that about the judge, but you're supposed to be a lady. But when I think—"

Mrs. MacTaggart reported resignedly, over the dishes, that the twins had cried themselves to sleep. "Sheepdogs, out in all weather they'll be, as you know. Hardy beasties."

The wind came howling around the side of the house and Alison said, "Yes, but—" But Luis would never *hear* of— She went into the living room and found him trying to settle down with *Actions and Reactions,* muttering occasionally about that warrant. She settled down herself with the latest Ursula Curtiss, and the wind howled, and her heart smote her.

"*Amante,*" he said.

Alison looked up. "*¿Cómo?*"

"It is," he said, "getting colder. I don't suppose—"

"What?"

"Well, *por Dios,* the damn dog belongs to somebody. Somebody else's property. If anybody ever does claim him, and he's contracted pneumonia or something—"

Alison laughed. "I really should know you better by this time. You do work so hard to cover up that awful softness—"

"I do not. I am not. All I said was—"

"Yes," said Alison. She found an old blanket, went out and folded it Cedric-size beside the washing machine on the service porch, and stepped out the back door, shivering. "Come on, boy. Too cold for idiot dogs out here tonight."

Cedric washed her hands, waggling his rump, while she untied him, and galumphed onto the service porch eagerly. "There's your bed, Cedric. Lie down. That's right. I hope," she added to Máiri as Cedric subsided with a thump, "he's housebroken."

"Now that," said Mrs. MacTaggart, "we will doubtless be finding out."

Apparently Cedric was housebroken. He was hustled out into the morning before the cats were up, but all four of them delayed going out in order to sniff long and thoroughly around the folded blanket.

Mendoza was still muttering about the judge. He got to the office late and was offered condolences by Hackett. "George was telling me. My God, Luis, he looks very good for it to me— almost the same M.O. As far as we've figured it. But we'll never get him if he is, unless we can look closer."

"*Como sí.* One of those things. And we'll have to let him go now," said Mendoza angrily. "Damn it, I'll be getting high blood pressure yet. So where to look?—back to Records."

"The routine," said Higgins. "But we can still sniff around Ackerman. Try to make him nervous. That kind, they're not just so stable to start with. If he is X, we might—"

"Where's the manpower, George? We have to go through the motions, the routine." Mendoza snapped his lighter. "We'll think about it. Especially if we don't turn up one more likely —or *as* likely."

But Palliser had had the inspiration on those punks, all right. "Why didn't I think of that?" wondered Grace. "What do you think, Lieutenant?"

"I think both of you should have thought of it yesterday. Go, go, check it out. We're supposed to be fairly smart detectives."

Hackett, Higgins, Piggott, and a yawning Landers started off to look over more known perverts out of Records, and Palliser and Grace set off for the Board of Education to ask questions about the corrective school where the troublemakers might have been sent. It was Glasser's day off.

The school was out on Vermont Avenue, the one for this area, and the principal listened to what they had to say, head on one side, and nodded, and said succinctly, "Henry Weiman, David Norbel, and Harry Naysmith. Yes. That poor devil of a grocer shot, I saw it in the *Times—that?* My good God. My good *God.* Those three young louts. All one can say." He was a sad man. "It's not that we don't try to do our best for these kids. We do. But what with the lax discipline in public school these days, and the lowered standards"—he shrugged—"by the time they get sent to us, it's really too late. So many factors. But it always goes back to the home, doesn't it? The family. Naysmith's father is in San Quentin. All the families on relief. My God—Naysmith and Norbel are sixteen, Weiman's fifteen. *Fifteen.* What do we offer? Too little, too late. Inevitably, it goes back to the home—the pattern set."

So there they were. Weiman wasn't at school; the other two were. But all minors, so there was a lot of red tape. The parents had to be contacted and talked to; they couldn't start talking to the punks, asking them any questions, until the parents knew, had had explained to them all the rights, and been offered the chance to get a lawyer there for the questioning. And maybe all that was right and proper—as Grace said to Palliser in the middle of it—only if so, it did seem as if Mr. William Blodgett, as representative of all the innocent victims, should have some representation there too. It really did.

It all took time. The principal let them use his office. They couldn't find all the parents at once; and when they did, Mrs. Naysmith was belligerent and a couple of others only too happy to make difficulties. Grace called in about ten o'clock to let Mendoza know what was going on.

It wasn't until a quarter of one that they finally tracked down Weiman, down the block from his home watching color television at the home of a neighbor who was also on relief. Grace and Palliser were starving, and they wanted to try to snatch some lunch before starting to question the kids.

It was Palliser who called in. "We'll be bringing them in now, Jimmy. Complete with parents and lawyers briefed to meet us. If the boss wants to sit in—What? *Oh, my God, no!*" There was naked shock in his voice.

"What's up?" asked Grace alertly.

They had fetched in four of them out of Records, and questioned them one by one. The unstable ones, the bad ones, with the incipient violence in them. It was the first place to look, but it didn't always turn up the jackpot. And Mendoza was still thinking about Ackerman. Lean on Ackerman some more? They'd had to turn him loose at 10 A.M.

They were all ready for lunch by a quarter to one, Mendoza chain-smoking, Hackett and Higgins grimly silent, and Piggott sitting back ruminating about the devil, when Sergeant Lake burst into the office and said, "Desk just called—there's another little girl missing from that school, same one Marla Pickens went to—she didn't come home for lunch—the mother called the school, she's there now, and no sign of the kid—"

"*¡Santa María!*" said Mendoza. They were all up, on the way, but he flung back at Lake, "Chase some squad cars up to Elysian—he used it before, could be he'll use it again!"

Chapter Eight

"I DIDN'T really begin to worry until it got to be twelve-thirty," said Mrs. Stark. She was in control, trying to keep her head, be of some help to them: a tall slender young woman with tawny-blond hair. "She always—Alice—comes straight home to lunch, and we're only over on Lucretia, it doesn't take her but ten minutes or so. I always have it ready at twelve-fifteen. I thought she'd been delayed somehow—and then—"

"Mrs. Stark," said Mendoza, "right now, quickly, if you'll tell us how your daughter was dressed, a general description —we want to get it out over the radio." This tense little group stood in the hall outside the principal's office at the elementary school. Mrs. Stark; the tall youngish principal, Mr. Ward, look-ing uneasy; Miss Grace Meade looking frightened; and the men from Homicide.

"Oh, yes. Of course. She's—Alice is eight, and about—about average size for her—She's got dark eyes and ash-blond hair. She had on a pink dress—bright pink Orlon, it turned so much cooler today, and a white cardigan—white socks and black shoes—"

Mendoza used the phone in the principal's office to relay that directly to Traffic. "We want some cars looking all around down here. We don't know this is the rapist, things could happen. But give it a try. And keep us informed at this number." As he went back to the group in the hall he tried to think, the innocent things that might have happened to Alice Stark. Did she cross an empty lot on her way home, maybe to fall and— Had some third-grade friend said, "Come home with me and see my new kitten," and that's right where she was now?

"—called the school, and the principal asked Miss Meade, but all she knew was that Alice had gone out of class at noon with the others—so I came—I walked over, looking for her all the way, but she wasn't—and little Susan said—she was just coming back after lunch, Susan, and she said Alice hadn't walked with her like she usually does—"

"Is she a responsible little girl, Mrs. Stark?" asked Hackett. "She's usually home on time? Doesn't forget the time and wander off?"

She turned to him a little blindly, having to adjust her vision, look up to find his face. "Oh, no. No, she's very good—obedient—about that. And—and she's so shy, it's worried me, but everybody said she'll grow out of it—only, I mean, she'd never talk to a stranger or—*Where is she?*"

And they couldn't reassure her, we'll find her, Alice is all right, because they were afraid she wasn't.

Grace Meade was pale. "Oh, not another one, it couldn't be," she said faintly. "I—the minute Mr. Ward told me, I tried to think, but there wasn't anything—different. Alice was in the last morning class, she left with the others when the bell rang. I didn't see her go out of the building, naturally, but Susan Hoff said Alice went out ahead of her and wasn't waiting to walk home—they go the same way."

It was ten minutes past one. The principal cleared his throat. "The rest of the children are all back in class now. If I might suggest—Mrs. Canelli can take your class, Miss Meade, if the police want to talk to you further—and I suggest that we have all teachers ask in class that any of the children who saw Alice at noon come to tell us about it."

"That's a good idea," said Miss Meade.

"She'd never have let a stranger pick her up," said Mrs. Stark in a trembling voice. "We'd warned her—but she's so shy anyway, she doesn't like strangers, and after all—after all," her eyes pled with Mendoza, "all residential streets here, people around—someone would have seen, if—it—was—that—one—that other poor child—oh, God, *where is she?*"

Miss Meade and the principal urged her into the office, to a chair. The principal said to Mendoza, "I'll get the word to all the teachers to ask about it in class. Something may turn up."

"Something!" said Hackett. They stood there for the moment with nothing to do, in the corridor redolent of the reminiscent odor of chalk, old wood, energetic young bodies, faintly of books. "How the *hell,* Luis? From a public schoolyard, all the other kids around? Because if she'd already started home, she'd have been with this kid she usually walked with."

"We don't know that. Maybe they'd had a little spat and she decided not to walk with Sue."

"It's only just over an hour," said Higgins. "We may all be having the jitters over nothing. All right, the mother says she's good, obedient. What else would the mother say? She could have gone home with another kid—or—"

"They're all back now, George. The ones who go home for lunch." There would be a few of those, maybe a good many: elementary schools scattered closer together for the smaller children, and within walking distance of many homes; and the school cafeteria would charge thirty, forty cents for lunch, money to be saved by going home. Some of the others would carry their lunches.

The principal came to them. "You'd better use my office to talk to the children—any who might have anything to tell you. This is—I pray it's not what it might be. My God, but it seems impossible—broad daylight—"

"Do you know the little girl, Mr. Ward?"

He shook his head. "I'm afraid not. Personally. It's a fairly large school, and my position is mostly administrative. I understand she's a good, quiet child—no trouble, no—my God. Broad daylight. It's something else. She lost track of the time, went home with another child or—" his voice trailed off.

"They're all back," said Landers.

"Did any of them see anything?" said Higgins.

Some had and some thought they had. There in the principal's office they listened to the few kids shepherded in by Miss

Meade. Sue Hoff. "No, we hadn't had a fight, honest, Miss Meade, only she wasn't there when I came out. She went out ahead of me, when I got to the door out into the yard I just couldn't see her anywhere."

A fourth-grader, Maria Fallow, looking bright enough, a little embarrassed by all the strange men. "I saw her in the yard, was all. I didn't *know* her, just knew who she *was,* you know. I saw her starting toward the gate on Le Moyne Street, I was going up to the cafeteria, it was just after the noon bell rang."

One of the third-graders in Miss Meade's class, Nancy Joiner, giggling and pleased at the attention. "She went out of class ahead of everybody. When the bell rang. Well, almost, I guess Tommy was first, he mostly always is. No, I didn't see her after that."

It would be slow, getting to all the kids. And the teachers—maybe one or two of them had seen her too. If not knowing Alice, seeing the pink dress. Somewhere.

The principal came in. "I thought I had better try to locate the father. He drives a city bus, I'm afraid there'll be difficulty reaching him—"

And none of the squad cars out cruising the area—or the others cruising Elysian Park—had made any report.

A brash sixth-grade boy, Jerry Niles, big for his age and awkward, Miss Meade looking at him doubtfully. "I seen that little kid, I can tell you, she got kidnaped right at the school gate, it was a big black man, he—"

"Jerry!" said Miss Meade. "This is serious. You know that's a lie. Now—"

"You cops," he said, staring at them. *"I'm* not scared o' cops. My big brother, he *shot* a cop once. He—"

Mendoza looked at him meditatively and said, "That was a lie, wasn't it? We don't need silly little boys cluttering up serious business. Out." The boy made a face at him as he left.

"Excuse me," said Miss Meade timidly, "but—I mean—when he's so disrespectful, and—and feels that way, maybe being more polite would—"

"Miss Meade," said Hackett, "it's too late. You can't change his attitude now." The phone rang on the principal's desk and Mendoza snatched it up.

"Mendoza. . . . Oh. Well, tell them to keep on looking." He put the phone down. "Report from the squad cars in the area. *Nada.*"

"Oh, I can't believe it's—" said Miss Meade, and the phone shrilled again. It was twenty-five past two.

"Mendoza. Yes, Jimmy . . . *Mil rayos,*" said Mendoza very gently. *"Sí . . .* Up by the—yes . . . *Yo tambié.* The lab truck, the works. O.K."

"Oh, my God, Luis, no," said Hackett.

Mendoza put down the phone. He looked remotely, coldly angry. He got up. He said, "They've found her. Up in Elysian. By the reservoir this time."

"Oh, no!" cried Miss Meade.

They looked at him. "Yes, dead," he said. "Very much like Marla." He took up his hat and turned to the principal. "I think you'd better try to get the father here before you tell Mrs. Stark. Or we can send up a policewoman—"

Ward nodded at him dumbly.

Another little girl missing from that school, and that was at the back of both Palliser's and Grace's minds; but they had their own job to do, here, with these young louts; they had to concentrate on that.

They'd taken half an hour to snatch some lunch, and by the time they got back to the office the lawyers were there, all from the Public Defenders' office. A dapper young Negro and two white men. The first hiatus arose over that, in the anteroom where the parents were waiting. The lawyers introduced themselves politely and the belligerent Mrs. Naysmith was shocked and voluble.

"I ain't gonna have no *nigger* for my boy's lawyer! Lawyer! What's a dumb nigger know about bein' a lawyer, for gossakes? I ain't puttin' up with it—"

The lawyer, a William Driscoll, looked slightly taken aback, and murmured to Grace, "Case of the pot and the kettle? No, wrong metaphor, I guess. A real live racist—don't know as I ever met one before." Grace grinned and said there were some still around. "I suppose I'd best go back and pick out a nice clean-cut Madison Avenue type for the lady."

In the end, that was just what happened, to save any more trouble; it was nearly three o'clock when Palliser and Grace faced the boys. The louts. With the lawyers sitting impassively by, a little bored, knowing their presence was completely redundant.

"All right, where'd you get the gun?" asked Palliser.

"What gun?" deadpanned Harry Naysmith, and brayed coarse laughter.

"The .32 you shot a man with, Harry," said Grace.

"Oh, we never do a real bad thing like that, mister," said Naysmith, making emphatic big eyes, smirking. He was the big one: sixteen, and what could you do with him now? The pattern set all right. Not a very bright boy, but also completely lacking in any of that thing called empathy: if you said to him, how'd you like that to happen to you, he wouldn't understand you any more than if you'd said it in Esperanto. The pattern: the father in Quentin, the attitude automatic, cops the enemy.

"Where's the gun, little boy?" asked Palliser coldly.

"I ain't—I—" That annoyed him.

Grace looked at the other two. Henry Weiman, David Norbel. Smaller, looking younger. The Weiman boy looking scared. "This was all Harry's idea, wasn't it?" he asked gently. "Kind of an exciting idea, and sounded like fun." Get down to their level.

"You guys shut up," said Harry. "I tol' you, never give the fuzz the time o' day—"

"And you'll keep quiet, little boy," said Palliser, "or wait outside."

"Did Harry have the gun, maybe?" asked Grace. Weiman almost nodded, stopped himself, looking confused.

"If you tell—damn it, I tol' you—"

Palliser stepped closer to Harry and said evenly, "If you had four cents' worth of brains, you'd know we had good reason to pick you up. You think everybody is blind, Harry? You think everybody's stupid? We've got a good witness who will probably be very prompt in identifying you—all of you—as the three punks who attempted that holdup and shot the clerk. You did know he's dead? We have witnesses from the other jobs you pulled, who will also identify you. I don't expect we'll have much trouble finding the gun, and the lab will prove it's the one killed the clerk. So you're just wasting your time talking. We know, Harry. It doesn't really matter a damn whether any of you says anything or not, you're all up for homicide. Understand?"

Harry's mouth opened. "Witnesses?" he said.

"Oh, God give me strength," said Palliser. One of the lawyers cleared his throat.

"Hey, m-mister, I and Dave d-didn't do no *murder* like you said. It w-was Harry had the g-gun," said Weiman, scared green. "It w-was—"

"You damn little fink—"

"All right," said Grace. "Outside." Palliser took Harry out, confused and angry, and Grace pulled up a chair and said, "You like to tell us about it, Henry?"

"S-sure. We didn't do no *murder*. It w-was Harry had the g-gun—it was one his d-dad hid away before he g-got sent up last time—an' he said, Harry s-said—it j-just went off, but I d-don't know, he been sayin' how he kind of w-wondered how it'd f-feel, shoot somebody—"

Grace and Palliser listened, and took notes, and the lawyers listened; and they felt tired. What were you going to do with this kind? Why did they come along, cluttering up things? No concrete answers: a lot of nice respectable friendly people in the poor down-at-the-heel sections of town, poor people: maybe mostly that kind. The Weimans and Norbels, followers: weak, maybe amoral, but not actively cruel, not aware of any principles good or bad. The Harrys—

"And we're not finished with him, are we?" said Grace. The louts had been booked into Juvenile Hall, and the parents and lawyers had gone away. Grace sat at his desk and lit a cigarette, contemplating the pages of notes to be transcribed; his regular-featured chocolate-brown face with its neat mustache looked a little drawn. "We'll be meeting Harry again. Maybe quite often, in time to come."

"I would take a bet," said Palliser. "Sixteen. He'll be stashed away at the sheriff's farm or somewhere until he's twenty-one, and then come up theoretically for sentencing. By which time everybody will have forgotten William Blodgett, and all too likely Harry'll be let loose. And commit more mayhem before he dies—or we get some realistic judges on the bench."

"All too likely." Grace got up and went to the door, walking rather heavily. "Jimmy. Did they find that little girl all right?"

"They found her," said Lake, looking sick. "Just like the other one. Up in Elysian Park. Dead. Raped."

"Oh, my God," said Grace quietly.

"I tell you, we were up here five minutes after we got the call," said the uniformed man passionately. "Four cars of us. We all went different ways, to cover the park—you see how the roads curve around up here, sir, but we *covered* it. There wasn't even a Parks truck up here. Nothing. The cars parked around the Academy, but that's all—"

A faint fleeting thought, a horrid little thought, struck Mendoza. One of the uniformed rookies in training. No well-brought-up little girl likely to distrust a policeman. *¡Disparate!* Those men all screened and tested every which way before they were accepted. "All right," he said. "He got hold of her—somehow—right then, right after twelve o'clock. When she started home. He brought her up here right away. He could be up here, in a car, in ten minutes. He could have raped her and killed her in another ten—fifteen—twenty. And been out of the park by twelve-forty-five."

Dr. Bainbridge got to his feet and looked down at the small twisted body. "Call it two hours to three," he said. "Just."

"What did I say?" said Mendoza savagely. "Twelve-fifteen to one-fifteen. He was away before any of you got here. Did any of you see anything on the way in? Pass a car, truck? At the entrances?"

The squad-car men all shook their heads. But it transpired

that none of them had entered the park by the Academy Road or Stadium Way entrances. "*¡Dios!*" said Mendoza. "He could have been on his way out as you came in."

"We didn't miss anything up here, I'll swear, sir," said the first man. "And it'd have taken an army to really search the place, only she wasn't—wasn't hidden. That pink dress—Darley spotted it right off when we came round that curve by the reservoir, she was out in plain sight up from the road—" he swallowed.

This was an even lonelier spot than the place where they'd found Marla. A wilder section of the park, where few people would ever come. Maybe not even the attendants. And as before, she had probably been raped and killed right here, at the foot of a young pine—the little scuffle marks, the blood. Her frilly pink panties torn and tossed aside. The pink dress torn. Her white sweater was missing: nowhere around.

All of them had looked once at her face—shy little Alice Stark—and then not again. She had been very frightened.

"God damn this bastard," said Bainbridge. "All right. You can take her in. I'll be down." He looked ferociously at the men from Homicide. "God damn it, haven't you got any leads at all? You'd better get off your asses and *find* this one, boys!"

"You like to have the job?" asked Higgins with sudden shocking ugly violence in his voice. "You like to help out on the damn routine? By God—"

"All *right*," said Bainbridge. "I know it's a bastard. But—" He made an angry, unfinished gesture and started down to his car on the narrow road below this gentle slope.

"Ackerman," said Hackett. "Can we say he's out? For—fifty percent sure? He was let out at ten this morning. And all right, they're unpredictable, but no jury or judge ever said he was insane. Or any head-doctor. He wouldn't go and do another right off the bat. Would he?"

"One thing we can say, Art," said Higgins, "it's the same one. Same as on Marla. No, I don't see Ackerman doing that."

"Why not?" said Landers. "He struck me as a very cool customer."

"What do you think, Luis?"

Mendoza was smoking, staring down at the little marks in the earth, the puddle of dried blood where Alice had died. He rocked a little meditatively, heel to toe. *"Pares o nones,"* he said absently. "That book. I keep going back to that book. *Learning Together.* Because—and also considering—I don't suppose Mrs. Stark will be in any state to be questioned tonight, maybe not tomorrow, but the father—Just possibly. Yes. Ackerman?" He stepped on his cigarette. "No, I think we can count Ackerman out. Just to be thorough, we'll ask him where he was, try to trace him after he left the Alameda jail this morning. But I think—on two counts—Mr. Ackerman is out."

"Two counts," said Piggott. "How come?"

"That book. Damn it, I must be woolgathering, because how could it be? How? Almost any other crime, but—"

"What are you talking about?" asked Hackett.

"All you smart detectives," said Mendoza. "I must be getting senile—if there was anything in it you'd have seen it too. All right, *¡vaya!* We'll all be doing some overtime. I want Ackerman checked, just in case. I want every man on that list from Records turned inside out—and we'll start now." He swung on his heel and started down for the Ferrari.

"But I did see her, Miss Meade. Honestly." Greta Larsen was earnest. "I never knew about it, about Alice, until Betty Jo stopped and told me on the way home from school, and then I remembered. And I told Ma and she said any way I could maybe help the policemen, I oughta do it, and even if the baby was still pretty sick, I better come and tell."

Grace Meade, about to drive herself home, hesitated here in the school parking lot. She knew Greta, who'd passed through her class three years ago; Greta was a sixth-grader. A nice polite girl, if no genius, and responsible. Greta, going home for lunch today, had been kept home to help with the sick baby, hadn't heard about Alice. But Greta was hardly the type to imagine things.

"Where did you see her, dear?"

"At the school gate. Out to Le Moyne Street. Do you think

she was *kidnaped,* Miss Meade? I saw her getting into a—a car."

"*Getting into a*—Are you sure, Greta?"

"Sure I'm sure. I saw her."

"But—do you mean she was just getting into a car by herself? There wasn't—wasn't anyone—pulling her, or—?"

Greta thought. "I think I remember somebody's arm sort of —sort of helping her. Maybe pulling her. Maybe. If she was kidnaped—"

"You're sure it was Alice?"

"I told you. Sure. Don't my little sister Trudy play with her all the time? I know Alice. And it *was.*"

"Well—what kind of car, Greta?"

Greta looked helpless. "Gee, I don't know. It was—it was—"

Miss Meade took the decision. "Well, anyway, for whatever it's worth I think you should tell the police. Would it be all right with your mother if I drove you to see them now?"

"Oh, gee, yes, Miss Meade. Ma said if I could help the policemen at all, I gotta. Because it's policemen protect all honest people."

"That's right, Greta. You get in, I'll take you to see them."

The twins were exuberant, having made the grown-ups back down. They had the promise, Cedric inside tonight too; it was threatening to rain. "Now don't bother Daddy," said Alison firmly. "He's worried. Please, Terry. Go with Máiri now, I *did* promise. When the cats are settled down—"

"*¡Todo el mundo* inside!" crowed Johnny.

"Really," said Alison to Mendoza, "they'll have to get English and Spanish sorted out before they start school, Luis. But how to do it—"

Mendoza grunted and got up, swallowing the last of his coffee. "You can expect me when you see me, *querida.*"

"I hope you get something," said Alison broodingly. Sheba jumped him as he went down the hall, and Alison came to pluck her off; she wasn't doing that as much these days. When the cats were settled, bring Cedric in. Not for the first time, she wondered what on earth they would do about Cedric if nobody ever did claim him. Crossing bridges . . .

Hackett called home to say they were working overtime. "I heard it on the news," said Angel. "This awful—Good luck, darling."

Higgins called home, still feeling astonished and proud and strange at having a home to call. "We'll be working overtime. Everything all right?"

"I heard about it on the news," said Mary. "George, how *awful*. That poor child. You catch him quick. Everything's fine. Stevie's trying to read *The Lay of the Last Minstrel,* he says he doesn't get it all but he likes it. Good luck, dear."

It wasn't often she said that, *dear*. Higgins felt better.

Palliser called home. "I didn't really expect you," said Roberta, "after hearing the news. This terrible—good luck on it."

Piggott, who had had a date to take Prudence Russell to dinner before choir practice, called to apologize. "It's this new homicide. Terrible thing, the little girl, and we want to get him fast if we can."

"Oh, Matt," she said. "I heard it on the news, it's awful. That poor little girl." Prudence was in the altos, and she had a deep warm voice. "Oh, good luck on it. I'll tell Mr. Gibbs why you aren't there. Matt—it makes you wonder that God lets such things happen. I mean, it's all very well to say Thy will be done, but God *couldn't* will such a terrible thing—"

"More like Satan winning one throw of the dice," said Piggott.

"Oh, *Matt,* what a way to put it. But—"

"But not the game, Prudence," said Piggott. "Never the whole kitty. We'll be on it. I'll see you Sunday."

"Yes. Good luck," she said warmly.

They found eleven men of the remaining list, up to midnight. Four of them had alibis for the crucial times today. The others were up in the air.

They checked out Ackerman, and at least cleared him off the slate. He said he'd taken a bus from the jail up to Holly-

wood, gone straight to his job; the manager of the office building had seen him there at five minutes to twelve. And this time
he hadn't had access to a car. Ackerman was out.

That was about all they accomplished on Friday night.

Saturday morning. Lake's day off, and Sergeant Farrell sitting on his desk. Farrell got shifted around, filling in for the
inside men on days off. It was a more usual February day, gray,
a little chilly, still the invisible threat of rain in the air.

Marla Pickens' funeral was scheduled for ten o'clock, at the
Hollywood Cemetery. Someone from Homicide might attend.

And Jason Grace said, putting on his jacket, ready to leave
the house at seven-thirty, "Maybe we're idiots, Virginia. I don't
know. Going to all the trouble and expense to, maybe, get to
be parents. Maybe have a little girl. To worry about. Warn
about the strangers, and if she's ten minutes late home from
school—Or the little boy. Worry like hell that he gets into bad
company—turns out wrong, however hard we try. You think
we're idiots?"

"We're idiots," said Virginia, smiling. "If there weren't a lot
of idiots around, Jase, everybody'd have stopped having children starting with Cain and Abel. Only *I* call them ordinary
optimistic people."

"All right," said Grace. "We're not idiots. I hope."

On the way to the office on Saturday morning, Piggott suddenly remembered those people they'd never talked to. What
was the name?—Sorenson. The other side of that old cut-up
house on the corner of Montana Street. The people out of
town for a funeral. Some one of them might—a long chance—
have seen Marla, on Thursday morning last week.

Was it worth checking back? If they were now home? Well,
just as well to be thorough.

And at seventeen minutes past eight, with all of them in
and thirty-three men out of Records still to be located and
leaned on, a new one was reported. The stationmaster of the
Union Station calling in, a body found in one of the rest rooms
over there, a lot of blood, a woman, and—

"Go see what it looks like, Jase—Tom," said Mendoza resignedly. "The rest of you—let's clean up this damn list today. And I'll offer odds it's N.G. *¡Santa María!* To hell with the hunch—where else to look?"

Chapter Nine

When Palliser and Grace got over to Union Station, an agitated man met them at the information booth: the stationmaster. "It's terrible," he said. "All the blood—and the major ladies' room in the building! I've got a sign up, but it's awkward—we've never had such a thing happen before. I don't know whether she committed suicide or what, but—it was Milly found her—"

"There'll be an ambulance along, sir," said Palliser. "They'll—"

"Yes, yes, Andrew here will direct them—" Still talking, he led them down the long wing to the left of the great main lobby. Benches, tables, tubs of sand, more benches, and a double swinging door labeled *Ladies*. Palliser reflected that cops get into a lot of places, but he couldn't recollect that he'd ever had to invade a ladies' room before. Yes, he had too—riding a squad car, that woman in sudden labor, and thank God the ambulance had come before—

There was a carpeted anteroom with a solid wall of mirror, a counter under it, chairs. Beyond another door, a long narrow tiled room, more mirrors on the right wall, basins underneath, wall cabinets dispensing paper towels. On the left wall, a row of toilet cubicles, the doors with a good eighteen inches of space beneath them, to the floor. But the details they didn't notice immediately; the body dominated the scene. And the blood.

The body was on the floor between one of the cubicles and the basins. And the blood—it covered the floor of that cubicle and an appalling area of the floor out here, and had seeped onto the floor of the cubicles on both sides. It looked like an abattoir. So *much* blood—In the middle of it, the body. A woman, with dark hair: about all you could say. Dressed, a dark skirt and blouse, the original color impossible to say: half under the door of the nearest cubicle, in the blood, lay a barely identifiable pair of panties and a half-slip. But Palliser and Grace saw instantly that she had been moved: some of the blood dry, some viscous, and a smeared trail from where the body now lay.

"You shouldn't have touched her," said Grace.

"Oh, dear, oh, dear, did I do wrong? I never meant to—I only thought, help the poor lady if I could—" She had come up behind the stationmaster, a plump, distressed-looking big black woman in a white uniform. "All that blood—I tried to keep my head, sir, lady took sick some way, look to me like maybe she had a miss right here, I just thought, help her—"

"Milly's the attendant here. Milly Jackson."

"Mrs. Jackson? How was she lying exactly? Where?" asked Grace.

"Right there in that toilet, sir, kind of sprawled out half over the stool—well—that is, one arm over it, like she tryin' to help herself up. I only thought—I only meant to do the right thing, try to help her—"

She had been dragged out, through the blood. None of it very fresh blood, but some fresher than the rest.

The interns came in. "Jesus!" said one of them. "What'd she do, cut her throat?"

"Well, what do you think?" asked Palliser.

They looked, heard the body had been moved, and one of them stepped fastidiously to touch the face, the neck. "It could be, on the very outside chance," he said, stepping back, "that she aborted here, spontaneously. But, barring complications, a female doesn't often go on and die of it. It's a lot better chance that she'd had an abortion within, say, twenty-four hours, and it was a botched job—very much botched—and she started a massive hemorrhage here—probably all of a sudden. Lost a lot of blood in a hurry, couldn't yell for help."

"Yes. How long has she been dead?"

The intern shrugged. "She didn't bleed to death in an hour. Your surgeon'll pin it down. Call it two, three hours. After maybe another two or three unconscious. Can we take her? Somebody'll have a job cleaning this place up."

Milly Jackson moaned. "Poor lady, poor soul. I only—"

Palliser looked at Grace. There would not very likely be any lab evidence to be found here. Just the blood. "Take her." They moved into the anteroom with the stationmaster and Milly Jackson.

"There was a handbag," said the stationmaster, distraught. "Milly gave it to me—" He nodded at the counter.

"It was under her, like she'd dropped it, when I started to pull her out, sir."

At that, not much harm done. The handbag was covered with dried blood, but it was a rough woven black straw, and wouldn't hold prints well. The flap was open. Palliser shoved it farther open and looked inside, saw a billfold, and lifted it out delicately between finger and thumb. Blue ostrich. He opened it. In the first plastic slot, a little I.D. card filled out. *Mrs. Jean Streeter,* an address on Genesee Avenue in Hollywood.

"Isn't there an attendant here at night?" Grace was asking.

"No, sir. We used to be jumping twenty-four hours a day, but since a lot of passenger trains are off, the station serves passengers only, of course, well, it just isn't necessary. Why, the crowds we used to get—" the stationmaster sounded wistful. "Milly is here eight to five, and that's it. The last passenger train out of here is eleven-forty, the Owl, and nothing else—no other passenger, that is—till the Daylight at eight-forty, so you see—"

"Then there wouldn't be many people around the station between about midnight and, say, six?" asked Palliser. "No station personnel even?"

"Not up here, sir. Oh, the cleaners—they'd be finished up here by about one A.M. Down in the baggage rooms and around the tracks—but not up here. Quiet as the grave after midnight or so."

"I see," said Palliser. "But the station's open? To the street?"

"Oh, yes, anybody could walk in. We get people coming in to use the public lockers, but not often after midnight. This woman—my God, she could have walked in here and never been noticed at all—"

The interns took the body away in a basket, and Milly Jackson moaned again. "Yes, well," said Palliser, "we'd better find out what we can about Jean Streeter. . . . You're looking pensive," he added to Grace as they went out to the lobby.

"You could say. It seems a little funny, woman inadvertently dying not to have the baby, when other people—and I don't know but what I still think we're idiots," said Grace.

With the rest of them out still chasing down the deviates out of Records, Mendoza took time off to attend Marla Pickens' funeral. Once in a while a murderer couldn't resist attending a victim's funeral. But it wasn't very likely here; and if he had attended, Mendoza couldn't spot him. Not many people there. A couple of reporters. . . . Since Alice, yesterday, there had been reporters, and not much to give them. . . . Mrs. Pickens was there, up toward the front: either no family room in this little chapel, or she'd chosen not to sit there. Neither of the other children there: another baby-sitter found, for next to her sat Rhoda Foster, looking smarter in a black dress, probably a girdle, and next to her a heavy-shouldered man, head down, who would be Frank Foster, in a plain dark suit. About fifteen other people, all strangers to him except Miss Grace Meade, looking pale. The others neighbors, probably: maybe some of the parents of children Marla had known. Paying respects.

The service was brief, and there was no graveside ceremony. As the Fosters, one on each side, supported a whimpering Mrs. Pickens toward the entrance, a reporter and cameraman came up, asked questions, snapped a flash-shot. Foster—heavy-jowled dark face, a man about thirty-five, sunken dark eyes in a square face—frowned and looked angry. His wife put a placating hand on his arm, and then turned and saw Mendoza. She dropped Mrs. Pickens' arm and took a hesitant step toward where he stood at the top of the aisle.

"It's that officer—you said, Lieutenant. I—I'd like a word with you, if you don't mind. I kind of thought about something you—" She turned back to her husband, who was still frowning after the reporter. "Frank, you take Margaret out to the car, I'll be along in a minute."

"What is it, Mrs. Foster?"

She was nervous. She looked at the last of the mourners filing decorously out, the officiating minister just disappearing through a side door. The coffin had been closed. "It was a nice service," she said, dabbing at her eyes. "Nice and simple. Right for a child—a little girl. I always wanted—but—I don't know but you'll think I was dumb not to think of it before, sir. I should have, maybe. But I never thought nothing of it at the time." She looked at him, and away. Her wonderful peaches-and-cream complexion glowed as she blushed slightly.

"What, Mrs. Foster?"

"Well, see, like we told you Marla and Eileen always come to me after school. Till about a quarter of five. And at times Marla'd go on errands for me. Loaf of bread, coffee, milk, like that, up to the store on Glendale Avenue. Or other things, at the drugstore or—And I been thinking, racked my brains when I first remembered it—I guess it'd be all of three, four months ago Marla first mentioned this fellow. At the market. Talkin' to her, and I seem to recall he got down somethin' for her she couldn't reach—I didn't ask her nothing about it, the market right there, people around, and Marla saying he was a nice man, joked with her and said her dress was pretty. But she wouldn't know good from bad, sir—I never thought, then. But now I recall, she did mention him three, four times again. She'd see him there at the market, the drugstore. Maybe six, seven times, altogether. Once she said he wanted to buy her an ice-cream cone, but she said no."

"Oh?" said Mendoza. "The market?"

"A little one just up on Glendale. Mr. Klamm's market. It's handy. I didn't think nothing of it, sir! People are nice to little kids lots o' times—say, what's your name?, or like that— and don't mean nothing by it. But now I *thought—*" she looked miserable. "If he was one like that, and maybe making up to her just so—"

"*¡Porvida!*" said Mendoza to himself. He rather liked this. It could fit very well. "Do you remember anything else she said about him? Did she know his name?"

"I racked my brains. I seem to get the feeling she called him some name, but not like Mr. Anything—it just don't *come*. I'm sorry. But I kind of seem to recall he had red hair."

"Think about the name. She called him—"

Rhoda Foster shook her head. "It's clean gone. It never crossed my mind was anything wrong about it—and maybe there wasn't, maybe he was just a fellow lives around there and likes kids. You know. I didn't pay much notion, her coming back from the store, saying the nice man was there again. Everything all right, broad daylight, Marla home all right. But now I think, it could've been—" She stared at him miserably. He pressed her for more, but that was it.

And he liked it. He liked it very much. He liked it so much that he drove out Glendale Avenue at once, and found the little market. He left the Ferrari around on a side street and came back. An independent general market, two storefronts wide, with the rack of newspapers outside the door. *Klamm's Market, Meats, Delicatessen, Fruits and Vegetables, Dairy Goods,* said the sign above the door. Mendoza also liked its location. It would be about seven blocks from Morton Avenue, about five from Lucretia.

A nice friendly man met casually on the errand to the market. The man friendly, not doing or saying anything bad. Seen, talked to, half a dozen times. And Alice shy, but—

No experience. No real judgment. And children tended to be literal about these things.

Mendoza had the sudden academic thought that it was a little short of miraculous that the race had got as far as it had:

every generation of kids starting out all new, so often reluctant to accept its elders' proscriptions.

He went into the market. Bins full of fruits and vegetables, a refrigerator case with milk, cream, ice cream, another with packaged meat, canned goods on the shelves round two walls at the back, where there was a counter and a cash register. An elderly spare man in a tan butcher's apron over a blue shirt and old trousers stood behind the counter. "Mr. Klamm?"

The man peered at him as he came up. "Nope. Just work here. Name's Barlow."

"Are you usually here in the afternoon?" Mendoza proffered his badge. "Just some questions, if you don't mind—"

Barlow peered myopically at the badge. "You're a cop. We never had no trouble here. What you want? I help out here, 's all. Afternoons, sure."

"Do you place a red-haired man, maybe a regular customer? Remember a little blond girl coming in, about three-thirty to four-thirty?"

Barlow shook his head. "I don't pay no attention to customers. Come in, dither around, don't know what they want half the time. Ask for soap powder or beans, right in front of 'em, they look. The kids is the worst. Imps of Satan, come in, knock things over, want six cents' worth o' candy. Anyways, I don't ordinarily wait on the people. I'm out back, unload stuff, stock the shelves, keep track o' what's sold. I'm only here helpin' out now, waitin' on people, account Ralph—Mr. Klamm—he's up in Frisco. Settlin' an estate. Old aunt of his died, I guess left him somethin' too."

"But do you—?"

"You ask Ralph, now, he could likely tell you. Hail fellow well met, like they say. Prob'ly knows ever'body comes in, regular. I don't." Barlow shrugged and turned to look suspiciously at a stout woman in tight blue stretch pants who had just come in. "Sorry. You come back when Ralph's here."

"And when will he be back?"

"Couldn't say," said Barlow. "You want somethin', ma'am?"

"I want some coffee—" she consulted a list.

"*On* the shelf you're standin' at, ma'am," said Barlow wearily.

"Jean's dead?" said the man. He sounded incredulous, not grief-stricken.

"That's right, Mr. Streeter," said Palliser. "I'm sorry to break bad news this way, but we'd like—"

"I can't say it's exactly bad news," said Wilbur Streeter. They had found him, it being Saturday, at home in the apartment on Genesee Avenue in Hollywood. He was a nondescript man of thirty-five or so, sandy, middle-sized, pug-nosed, round-shouldered. "I won't lie to the police. No. I'm just surprised. Was it an accident?"

"Well, not exactly," said Palliser. "She was your wife? This address was still in her billfold—"

"Oh," said Streeter. "You better come in and sit down." Palliser and Grace went in. It was an old apartment, but looked neat and clean. A portable television set was mouthing silently in one corner, an old movie, and Streeter went over and shut it off. "I get you anything to drink? Beer, coffee?"

"No, thank you, sir," said Grace. "Mrs. Streeter—"

"Yes. Well, I've got to tell you, we never did hit it off. I didn't expect any angel, gentlemen, I get married. No. But I did figure on having, you know, a nice place. Home. Maybe a couple of kids. Dinner ready when I get home—I'm a book-keeper, at Bullocks' downtown. You know. And on that we didn't see eye to eye, if you get me. *Was* it an accident?"

"No," said Palliser. "It looks as if she had an illegal abortion and it turned out a botched job."

"Oh," said Streeter. "Oh. Well—poor Jean. She was thirty-three, but it was like she never grew up. Never got over wanting to go out somewhere every night, the dancing, the bars, the —she couldn't cook and she wouldn't keep house." It was an old story. "I tried to be patient with her, I don't like rows, but there it was. We were married four years back and I was fed up the first six months, but—" he shrugged. "A divorce costs, and God knows I hadn't an eye on anybody else. Lucky we didn't have any kids, tough on them. She walked out about, oh, seven, eight months back. I haven't seen her since. Didn't especially care to. So she got caught, did she, and—Poor Jean."

"Do you know where she was living?"

"I can only tell you what she told me when she walked out. She was going to this old girl-friend's place, a Doris Graham, stay with her. No, she never said anything about a divorce. Why should I take the trouble? I wasn't about to take the gamble again."

"Mr. Streeter, we've got to have formal identification of the body," said Grace. "Could you come down and make that?"

Streeter said, "Sure. If I got to. I guess it's the least I can do for her. Poor Jean."

"And I like it," said Mendoza dreamily. "I like it very much indeed. I'd been thinking along similar lines myself. The nice man with red hair." He had unprecedentedly ordered a highball and was sipping it meditatively.

"You'd never heard of him until—oh," said Higgins.

"He always likes them offbeat," said Hackett sourly.

"It fits in so much better, Arturo," said Mendoza. "The personal touch." He had come back to the office to find Hackett and Higgins just at loose ends after leaning on the latest deviate from Records, and they were foregathered at Federico's over an early lunch. "That book was the first thing that struck me. Really now, if Marla had been accosted by a stranger on the street, dragged into a car—fortuitously nobody noticing—she would have dropped that book, wouldn't she? All right, if not in the street, in the car. He'd probably have had to knock her out, and she'd certainly have dropped the book. And then there's Greta Larsen."

"A twelve-year-old," grunted Hackett. "Maybe wanting a little attention. Get in on the excitement."

"No imagination," said Mendoza. "Even to make up that simple little story. She saw Alice get into a car. Outside the schoolyard gate. *Naturalmente*. I do wonder if Alice used to run errands for her mother up to that market too."

"Yes. So do I," said Higgins. "We can ask."

"Shy Alice—same like in the song," said Mendoza somnolently, " 'who wept in delight when you gave her a smile, and trembled with fear at your frown.' Instead of dropping the book, Marla had hung onto it all the way up into the park. Hung onto it getting out of the car, only let go of it, maybe, when the nice man began acting not so nice. And Alice, shy Alice, climbing into a car. It just makes it easier, Art."

"Oh, I see it, I see it. You're miles from proving it, and light-years from finding him, but—"

Mendoza sat up and sipped his drink. "I don't know that. And I'm not saying it *was* the nice red-haired man at the market. It could well have been. We'll go looking for him. The fellow who was friendly, asked Marla's name, offered her ice cream. And didn't do or say anything wrong. Then. Marla, on her way back to school that morning, probably wouldn't have hesitated to get into a car if that one came along and offered her a ride. She knew him. In a way. He was familiar—in a way. He'd been—mmh—nice. Yes. And if shy Alice had run into him at the market too—or around there, there's also a drugstore, a hardware store—ditto for her. But this says something else to us. . . . I never thought we'd get him out of Records."

"You just like them complicated, *as* I've said before," said Hackett.

"Very uncomplicated, Arturo. We've said that most little girls in the big city are warned about the strangers, these days. *Pues sí.* But they aren't warned, because parents never think about it, against the familiar strangers."

"The—"

"All sorts of them," said Mendoza. "Oh, bring me the steak sandwich, Adam. . . . The mailman. The fellow at the service station where Daddy always takes the car. The male checker at the supermart where Mommy shops. The druggist in the corner store. The bakery-truck driver coming around, Mommy buying from him. The insurance man coming to the house. The landlord. The man to fix the refrigerator. The driver of the Good Humor truck. The—¡*Ca!*" said Mendoza. "Judgment? It wouldn't occur to the eight-year-old to think of a man known like that as a stranger. The bad stranger she's been warned about. She *knows* him. He's placed."

"Now you just might have something there," said Higgins. "I see it."

"Borderline," said Mendoza. "Neither one thing nor the other. As far as an adult is concerned. And all those men, subject to the human passions and deviations even as everybody else. But the child not knowing that. A known face, not the sinister stranger."

"Yes," said Hackett consideringly. "Enough to give him the edge. Just the time needed to get them willingly into the car. With no fuss."

"*Facilimente.* Now I'll tell you. I like this red-haired fellow at the market. That clerk says the owner, Klamm, knows everybody coming in regularly. Absolutely nothing says that the fellow ever approached Marla in Klamm's hearing or sight. But we'll ask him about the fellow—*condenación,* when he gets back. We—"

"Meanwhile, go house to house for blocks around looking?" asked Hackett.

"You will be facetious. I want to know whether Alice ran errands up there too. And," said Mendoza, "let's try to build up a little list of the men those little girls might have known —as the familiar strangers. In a fashion. As well as the parents can tell us."

"Familiar strangers," said Higgins. "You may indeed have something there, Luis." And he was thinking that the people next door to the house on Silver Lake Boulevard had a regular gardener, Laura would know him, and Mary sent her on errands to the drugstore up a few blocks, there might be a dozen men Laura knew casually—in a fashion—that he and Mary didn't know a damned thing about. You didn't think—

"An ab——Oh, my God!" said Doris Graham. "Jeanie *dead* —like that. My God. It was that bastard, that Huddy Bell! It musta been—got her into the fix, and then took her to some butcher—I never did like that guy, but she couldn't see—"

"Bell?" said Palliser.

"Sure, sure, I'm telling you—Hudson his name is, but every-body calls him Huddy—Jeanie's boyfriend, since she left that creep Streeter. My God, Jeanie dead." Doris Graham, defiantly henna-haired and purple-lipsticked, produced a sob. "It was awful bad luck, her getting caught like that. And now some quack—Well, sure I knew about that, she was good and mad. I suppose she went and told Huddy, anyways she told me it was all fixed up, to get rid of it, and she—but I don't get this, did you say Union *Station?* What'd she be doin' there? She told me it was all fixed, she left here last night about seven, said Huddy was goin' to pick her up and take her to this place, and she'd stay over till Sunday. You go ask Huddy, he's the one did it. Take her to some butcher—What? Well, he works at a men's store out Fairfax, the Savoy, Savile—"

"Would you say lunch before we find Huddy?" suggested Grace. "I wonder how the other boys are doing on the deviates. I hope—"

"I don't know, Jase," said Palliser, "that I think the routine will turn this one up. The Lieutenant kept saying, that book. I think I've got what he meant."

"I saw that, but it's impossible," said Grace. "A thing like this. Somebody the little girls knew—For one thing it was the same boy on both of them."

"Oh, yes," said Palliser. "That's what makes it look so— Lunch, I guess. Before Huddy. What the hell are we doing, wasting time on poor Jeanie? No loss to society."

"The ninety and nine, as Matt would say. We do seem to be committed to upholding the law and order."

Over a sandwich at a drugstore, Piggott said to Glasser, "We never did see those Sorensons. They were out of town. Corner of Montana there. I suppose we should check back."

"I suppose. But it's a week and two days ago, on Marla. Would anybody remember? We've still got six of these out of Records to find, Matt."

"Well, we're supposed to be thorough, Henry."

"Sure, sure." Glasser finished his coffee and sighed.

The next one on the list—they had brought two in for

Landers and Higgins to question—was on Blanchard Street in Boyle Heights, one Clyde Engel. They drove over there in Glasser's car. It was an old frame house, two-storied, with a sign in the front window, *Room for Rent*. The woman who answered the door was mountainously fat and smelled of sweet wine. "Engel?" she said. "Him. Didden you know? He passed away last week. City had t' bury him, he didden have nothin'."

"So at least one of them's gone to judgment," said Piggott. "What's the next one, Henry?"

"Highland Park," said Glasser dispiritedly.

"What?" said Hudson Bell, outraged. "Me! Me? That damn Doris—You're telling me Jeanie's *dead?* Like that? My God— but I—Listen, I don't know a damn thing about it! I didn't even know she was—she never told me. I swear I—Look, I got a decent job here, I can't afford to be mixed up—That Doris!" He stared at Palliser and Grace, a weakly handsome young fellow, looking scared and mad. "Look, I used to run around with Doris some, before I met Jeanie. She just wants to get me in trouble, that's all. I never knew Jeanie was p.g.—she never said a word. And it wasn't like, I mean, I guess she went out with other guys too. I do know she'd had one before —she told me that—before she got married to that guy. An abortion, I mean. But I never—What'd Doris *say?* Last night? My God, I was visiting my mother in the hospital, she's just had an operation, the French Hospital on College it is—you can check—I was there the whole visiting time, with my sister and her husband—the nurse can say! My God, I can't take it in about Jeanie—but, it happened that way, she fixed it up her-self—I don't know a damn thing about it. I don't—"

Palliser and Grace went down to the French Hospital and saw, in that order, the special nurse and Mrs. Flora Bell. Hudson Bell had indeed been there last night, from seven to eight-thirty, visible all the while. With Mrs. Bell's daughter Florinda and her husband Gilbert Fletcher.

It was two-forty.

"I guess we go back and see Doris again," said Grace.

"I guess we do," said Palliser. "The stupid little people telling lies. I get fed up, Jase."

"We all get fed up. But we have to do the job. I do wonder what they're getting on that. That's the important one right now. We're just cleaning up the flotsam."

"Poor Jeanie," said Palliser.

Bast had reached the conclusion that whatever the stranger was, he posed no danger at all. He was foolishly friendly, allowing his food to be stolen, and he was foolishly gentle with the small humans, letting them maul him. That sort of thing no self-respecting cat would put up with.

He smelled of Dog, unself-respecting Dog, the fawner on humans, but he did not altogether behave like Dog. At any rate, he was harmless.

Bast waited until the small humans had vanished into the house, as they always did in early afternoon, and got up and stretched leisurely, and approached the stranger.

For once he did not wriggle and whimper, *Friends, please be friends.* He stayed still, only rolling one eye at her now and then, and quivering senselessly.

Bast smelled him all over, the foolish stranger, and there was quite a lot of him to investigate. Not all Dog. There was a faint, long-ago smell of cat—especially at the ears—and Bast gave one ear an absentminded lick. The stranger uttered a low word of gratification.

There was, in fact, a good deal more ear to get one's teeth into than with any of her offspring, and Bast chewed meditatively for a moment before going on to the whiskers. A long while back, a cat was present there too.

Friends, he said.

Food stolen, of course, always tasted better.

He began to wash her ears, gently. Bast always enjoyed being washed, and so far forgot herself as to utter a purr. Cats washed cats. She curled her front feet under and shut her eyes, enjoying the pink tongue.

El Señor's loud hiss opened her eyes. He was properly swelled for danger, tail stiff as she had taught him, and Sheba beside him arched, claws out. She spoke to them softly. The stranger had no sense—not being all cat—and could undoubtedly be useful. More hamburger. And another willing tongue for washing.

Chapter Ten

"What?" said Roy Stark. "What did you say? I'm sorry, I'm not—Marian wanted me to take some of the stuff the doctor gave her, but I guess you've got to face up to—I don't mean Marian—thank God she's out, at least she can sleep—" He passed a hand over his face, a stocky man turning bald early; not ranting or raving, but there was deep grief and deep anger in his bloodshot blue eyes. "When she was the only one—I'm sorry. Any way I can help you—find him. What did you—?"

"Was Alice ever sent on errands up to the stores along Glendale Avenue?" repeated Mendoza.

He nodded. "Oh, sure. Sometimes. Saturday afternoons, and after school. There aren't any main streets to cross, the market's on this side of—Every now and then she'd be sent, or go up there to spend her own money, ice-cream cone, like that. I—I remember she liked the man who runs the market. She was so shy, you know, until she got to know people, but—"

"Mr. Klamm, who owns the market?"

"I don't know his name. I don't think Alice did."

"Did she ever mention another man she met up there, who was nice and friendly, talked to her? A man with red hair?"

Stark shook his head. "I never heard—do you mean it was some guy *there*? That—?"

"We don't know, Mr. Stark," said Hackett. "We're just looking everywhere."

"Sure," he said tiredly, "sure. A guy at the—No, I never heard her say about anything like that. Maybe Marian did, maybe she'd remember. I'll ask her when she's awake. But you know, Alice was so shy with people, I don't think it's likely she'd have—"

The wife might know better. Might remember something. They began to ask about the other familiar strangers, and Stark looked bewildered but answered docilely. No, they didn't use a laundry service, Marian didn't buy from Helms Bakeries, or—

They didn't get much from him. They hadn't got much from Mrs. Pickens either. Mrs. Pickens at the Foster house, a sagging old California bungalow on Morton Avenue. The Foster house, thought Mendoza, was a study in contrariness. Everything shabby and very untidy—it was no wonder Rhoda Foster hadn't been sure about the schoolbook, a very indifferent housekeeper to say the least; but a feeling of warmth and welcome and comfort in the place. "Frank had to go back to work, he was sorry—and I hope you won't hafta disturb Margaret any way, she's awful low in her mind." But they didn't get across to her what they were after at all. She could, after remembering him, envisage the friendly man at the market as possibly a villain, but the idea of other kinds of familiar strangers didn't penetrate. "What you *mean?*" she kept asking. "I don't know—well, I don't buy much at that store, it's usually higher and—But people we *know,* acquaintances like you say, none o' *them*'d be anybody like this fiend— what you mean?"

All they got there was the names of Marla's best girl friends, Jane Wilanowsky and Sandra Kreisleer.

"So it is possible," said Mendoza on the way back downtown. It had started to rain slightly. "Alice ran errands up to the market too. My God, Art, I wonder about Klamm? The owner?"

"That other fellow said he was out of town—"

"Yes, but for how long? Is he really? But one thing at a

time," said Mendoza. "The red-haired man may have been nice and friendly to Alice too."

"And how do we go about finding if he was?"

"Kids," said Mendoza. "Little girls. They sometimes tend to chatter more to their friends than to parents."

Piggott and Glasser had brought in another one from Records, good sheepdogs separating the black from white, and Higgins and Landers were questioning him. One Claude Kitchins, the expectable record, said Sergeant Farrell laconically. Mendoza opened the door of the interrogation room.

"—the best you can do, Claude? 'Just around'?" Higgins' deep voice.

"That's the best I can do." Sullen, unwilling. "How'd I remember? I go here 'n' there. I got to report to the P.A. officer, I don't want no trouble, get back in. I ain't done nothin'. I told you."

"But you don't remember where you were yesterday at noon?" Landers.

"No, I don't. Why should I? Around somewhere."

Mendoza shut the door. "Around and around," he said. "So many of them, what good to find them and ask? Up in the air!"

Palliser and Grace plodded in, both looking tired and disgusted. "This is all a handful of nothing," said Palliser, and sat down at his desk and lit a cigarette. "If you want to hear an edifying story we can tell you about Jeanie. The female at Union Station."

"Oh, yes. What about her?" Mendoza and Hackett followed them into the sergeants' office.

Palliser started to tell him. Grace just sat back and shut his eyes. "And so Doris admits, when she knows Huddy has an alibi, that Jeanie didn't say it was Huddy had fixed up the job, was picking her up—Doris doesn't know where Jean was going for the job, just that she was. And so what? We can piece it together—a botched job, and she died of it, but where she went, to whom, who's to say? And what was she doing in Union Station?"

"Sometime after midnight—not much after midnight," said

Mendoza. "On her way home, maybe, felt sick, or started bleeding, and went to the nearest—" Mendoza shrugged.

"But she did say she'd be staying over Sunday. Wherever she went. Why did—?"

"Yes," said Mendoza absently. "Jase—"

"And somebody did pick her up last night."

Grace sat up and opened his eyes. "No rest for the wicked."

"Our soft talker," said Mendoza. "Go see the little girls, Jase. See what you pick up. On the red-haired man."

"Reverting to Sherlock Holmes now."

"*Por Dios,* I forgot you hadn't heard all—" Mendoza gave a brief outline, and Grace looked interested.

"That could be something indeed. Even odds the market owner could place him. But the other little girls—"

"Little girls," said Mendoza, "playing together. Chattering together. Telling each other things. Even if—mmh, yes—one of Marla's friends, Alice's friends, didn't happen to go running the errands together with them. Go see, Jase. If there's anything there at all. We might hit a jackpot."

"I suppose I'd better start getting out a report on Jeanie," said Palliser with a groan. He pulled his tie loose, drew his chair closer to the desk, and slowly rolled a triplicate form into the typewriter. "Equal before the law people may be, but not otherwise. I kind of resent the time wasted on Jeanie. Who was no loss."

Grace got up. "Let me have the names and addresses." As he went out to the anteroom, Piggott and Glasser, looking rather wet, were shepherding in another one, a big sloppily dressed man in his fifties, who was complaining loudly, "Ain't I got any rights? I done the time, I'm out five years, I ain't done nothing else, I don't know why you guys got to—"

"Just a few questions, Walter," said Glasser. "In here."

It was raining a little harder, as if it were trying to work up to a real storm. By the time Grace got to the Larsen address on Delta Avenue, it was coming down steadily. Twelve-year-old Greta Larsen, who had said she'd seen Alice getting into a car at the schoolyard gate yesterday noon, had earnestly added that Ma said you ought to help policemen, so Grace didn't anticipate any difficulty here getting whatever was to be got, and he was right.

Mrs. Larsen, large, motherly, blond, and exuding warmth as her kitchen gave forth the smell of fresh-baked bread, welcomed him in calmly. "Whatever my children can tell you that you wish to know, sir, they will. About the poor little one. My Trudy played with. A nice little girl. It makes the heart heavy to think."

"Yes, ma'am," said Grace. "Is Trudy here?"

"In the kitchen. The cookies just come from the oven—you try." She led him back there, to a large square kitchen where the two little girls, twelve and eight, sat at a large square table with cookies and milk. "I go see to the baby. This is a policeman, girls, to ask again about the little Alice. You tell what he ask, if you know." She gave Grace a plate of warm cookies and a benign smile and went away. The little girls looked at him with round-eyed respect and interest.

He sat down across from them and absently started to eat a cookie. "Trudy," he began in his warm voice, "you played with Alice a lot, didn't you?"

She nodded, a pretty, very blond little girl with pigtails and large blue eyes. "Yes, sir. All the time. At school, sometimes at Alice's, and here."

"Does your mother send you on errands up to the store sometimes? Up to the stores on Glendale Avenue?"

"Sometimes. Mostly it's Greta, but if she isn't here, me."

"Did Alice do that too? For her mother?"

"Sometimes. Sure. Sometimes I went with her."

"Um," said Grace comfortably, finishing the cookie. "Did she ever say anything to you about meeting a man at the market there, somewhere around? A man with red hair, who was—you know—nice to her?"

Trudy looked surprised. "Why d'you want to know about him for? Alice liked him—you know, she was an awful scaredy-cat about people she didn't know, a real baby, she was funny about people." Eight years old, not comprehending death, accepting it: not quite sure what had happened to Alice; she was matter-of-fact. Grace waited for it. "But she wasn't scared of him. After she got to know him."

"The red-haired man. She told you about him?" Greta was listening with round, serious eyes.

"Um-hum," said Trudy. "She told me he was nice. A funny man. He could do magic tricks, make things disappear like a real magician. After she got to know him, she liked him, and sometimes he'd be at the market, or somewhere up there, when she went."

"Did you ever see him, Trudy?"

She shook her head regretfully. "It was only sometimes he'd be there when she was. Buying things for himself, I guess. Alice just told me about him."

"Does Mr. Klamm know him?—the man at the market?"

"I dunno," she said vaguely. "Alice just said she always hoped he'd be there if she went up, because he was funny and made you laugh."

"Do you know his name, Trudy? Did Alice know—?"

She looked surprised again. Sometimes, it must seem to the kids, he thought, that grown-ups knew everything, and it was a revelation to find they didn't. "Why, sure! He was Mr. Sam."

"Mr. Sam," said Grace. "Just Mr. Sam?" She nodded. "Do you know when Alice first met him there?"

"Oh, gee, a long while ago. Way last semester it was, she said—"

"Before Christmas?"

"Sure, before Christmas." Her eyes were curious on him.

"That all you can tell me about him?"

"It's all I can think. Except I never met him and I'd like to. I like magic tricks."

Grace finished his second cookie and looked at Greta. "You ever hear about this Mr. Sam?"

"No," said Greta, "and I'm surprised Alice would—a *stranger*, like Ma's always saying be careful—And you just stay away from him if you do see him there." She looked at Trudy severely. "Do—do you think he was the one—?"

"We don't know, Greta." Mr. Sam. Well.

"I didn't see anybody in the car she got into—but there was somebody, because it drove right off."

"About that car," said Grace. "The car you saw Alice get into—can you tell me any more about it? The color?"

"It was white. I said that." She was hesitant. "I—I don't know much about cars. Brands."

"Sedan? Convertible? Big car or little?" He smiled encouragingly at her.

"I don't know what that is. It was sort of medium size. But it wasn't like a regular car. I don't know how to say it—I seen them, but I don't know what the name is for them. Like—just a front seat where the driver sits and then no back seat, just a —just long sides and no top on the back. Where you can put things to carry them. I don't—"

Grace stared at her. "Like a little truck, Greta? Like that?"

"Yes," she said. "Like that."

Well. A pickup truck. White. "Did it have a sign on the door? Any name? Lettering?"

"They asked me that before. I don't remember. I'm sorry. I—I didn't think nothing about it then."

But that was something—two somethings—they hadn't known before.

It was raining a little harder by the time he found Sandra Kreisler. There wasn't anybody at home at the Wilanowskys' house on Quintero, but at the Kreisler's on Kellman everybody was home, including a small boy practicing a piano lesson and a small feisty mixed terrier who snapped at Grace's ankles. Mrs. Kreisler, after taking a long look at his badge and accepting him as a bona fide police officer, would have talked at length about these awful murders, the innocent children, and the dangers of city life; he cut her off politely. "If I could talk to Sandra, Mrs. Kreisler?"

"Oh, I suppose. I'll go get her. You'd better use the den. Benny's loud, whether he's good or not."

Sandra was dark instead of blond, and inclined to self-importance because she'd been Marla's best friend, but what he got there backed up Trudy. Oh, that man? Sam his name was, Marla'd talked about him. At the market, sure. She'd met him there first a long way back. Yes, before Christmas. "Only we don't have Christmas, it's Hanukkah."

"Sure," said Grace. "Before December?"

"I guess. Last semester. She said he did magic tricks and made you laugh. She liked him, but it wasn't very often he was there."

Grace thought, yes, but probably not very often the little girls were there either. The red-haired man could easily be a regular customer, be living somewhere around there. Sam. Mr. Sam. He was beginning to feel very interested in the red-haired man as a very hot lead, and he went back to the office to pass all that on to Mendoza. It was then four-fifty and still raining.

"*¡Vaya!*" said Mendoza, listening. Hackett, Higgins and Landers were sitting around the office too, another possible having just been let go. The autopsy report on Alice was in: sounding much the same as Marla's. "So there we are. I like him. I like him very much."

"If he's a regular customer there this Klamm will know him," said Grace. "Place him by the red hair, I should think. Not so common after—"

"*¡Carape!*" said Mendoza. "I know it. I have been back to the market. That old idiot Barlow hasn't any idea where Klamm's staying in San Francisco. Didn't think a hotel. Had an idea, home of the old aunt, or whoever it was who died. Can't say what her name was. There's no damn way to contact him. If he should come home tomorrow—"

"Frustrating," said Higgins. "I like the sound of him too. Just the way you said, the kids—somebody they knew casually like that. Even shy little Alice."

Hackett felt his eye. Since Wednesday it had developed beautifully and up to yesterday had presented all colors of the rainbow, but it was fading now. "And of course we can't just drop all the other possibles," he said. "Though I like him too. And another thing about it, Luis, this funny man who does magic tricks—both little girls warned about strangers, so maybe they didn't say much about him at home because they knew they'd be told to stay away from him, and they liked him by then. It's something, all right. . . . I understand you're still stuck with the mysterious pooch. Angel said—"

"*¡Por Dios!*" said Mendoza. "For my sins, these things happen to me. A shaggy dog, my God. And the ad's been running for five days. All I can think is—" The irresponsible careless people.

"A dog?" said Landers.

"A large shaggy dog. In my wife's car last Monday morning. Cedric, *caray*. And nobody—" Mendoza put out his cigarette. "Now, just in the event that nobody ever does claim him, which of you would like, for free, a well-trained purebred watchdog? Guaranteed young and strong—"

"Now really, Luis," said Hackett. "You know we've got a cat. You wished him on us yourself."

"Afraid not," said Grace. "We haven't got a fenced yard."

"Brucie'd never let him past the gate," said Higgins.

"I'd like a dog," said Landers, "but living alone, it wouldn't be fair to the dog. Especially a big dog."

"So, get married."

"Just to have a dog? I'm not that much of a gambler," said Landers.

"But damn it," said Mendoza, "Alison won't take him to the pound. And my cats—damnation." He picked up the autopsy report again. "The inquest is set for Tuesday. Inquest on that Sutcliffe tomorrow. We haven't had a formal I.D. on him yet."

"That sergeant from Fresno phoned," said Hackett. "The sister'll be here tomorrow."

They'd be doing more overtime tonight, with Galeano and Schenke, continuing to find the possibles. But they were now all more interested in the red-haired man, and it was frustrating not to be able to follow that up.

Just on the off chance, Mendoza stayed late at the office to send wires to every hotel in San Francisco, and on second thought every funeral director, making inquiries for Mr. Ralph Klamm. If those turned up any information, it would be tomorrow.

When he got home, through the rain driving down in earnest now, Alison met him at the back door. "I didn't want you to have a heart attack, *querido*. Break it gently."

"What? Why?" He took off his hat and kissed her.

"Look," said Alison, and stepped aside.

"I don't believe it," said Mendoza, having looked. *"Incredíble!* My grown-up sensible Bast—"

There on the folded blanket beside the washing machine was the large shaggy dog Cedric. He was looking proud and pleased, insofar as any expression could be seen behind his face-veil of hair. And there between his large furry front paws, feet folded under her, eyes shut tight, was Bast. Cedric was washing her ears with his long pink tongue, making slurping sounds.

"I do *not*—"

"Did you ever see the like?" demanded Mrs. MacTaggart. "A cat raised with a dog, 'twould be no surprise, but that selfish-hearted Abyssinian creature—"

"It was a surprise to the others," said Alison. "They were incredulous too. It was Bast stole Cedric's dinner this time."

Cedric suddenly noticed the newcomer, made an apologetic noise, got up, and offered a courteous paw.

"Somebody," said Alison, "has trained him. I cannot imagine—"

"It is a mystery all round," said Mendoza. "All I can say. A deep dark mystery, *cara*. And I'm only a workhorse cop, I am not used to mysteries, or equipped to cope with them."

"The offspring are simply delighted. They've got it quite decided between them," said Alison rather nervously, "that Cedric is—um—permanent. Luis—"

"Bast or no," said Mendoza, "this is my house, and I do not want a large shaggy dog in it."

"Well, but, Luis—"

"The man will be hungry," said Mrs. MacTaggart in her most Scottish voice, and went back to the kitchen. Cedric lay down again and licked Bast's head thoughtfully. Her purr swelled and she began to make rhythmic bread against him, claws going in and out in his long tangled chest ruff.

"¡Prepóstero!" said Mendoza.

It was still raining on Sunday morning, a thin dispirited drizzle coming down monotonously. There had been no responses to Mendoza's wires to the funeral homes, but all the hotels had replied: no Ralph Klamm registered.

Nine o'clock brought Mendoza Miss Anita Sutcliffe and her fiancé, Dr. Larry Clifford. "I just couldn't bring myself to come without Larry—knowing Martin was—and that sergeant said it was just the formal—but it's no good crying, I've got to be sensible. Only it's such a—wanton thing, isn't it?" She was a pretty girl, auburn-haired. "Martin was so good. And just because this criminal—just at random—happened to—It doesn't make sense. It just doesn't make sense."

Cops saw a lot of things that didn't make sense, but Mendoza didn't say so to her.

"I couldn't get off till last night," said Clifford. "I'm interning at a local hospital. But I thought I'd better do the formal identifying. Do you know when the inquest will be?"

"Tomorrow, ten A.M., I'll give you the address." And on Tuesday, the inquest on Alice Stark. It would be very nice to be able to offer further evidence on that, but the way it looked now—

The red-haired man. Sam. Mr. Sam. And—seized with sudden doubt, Mendoza wondered—would Klamm know him? If the red-haired man had been deliberately setting up the little-girl victims—At the market, said the little girls, but did that mean *in* the market? Not so necessarily. Reading a newspaper off the stand just outside, joking with the little girls, doing his magic tricks—oh, yes? Would Klamm ever have seen him?

Even that was all up in the air.

And if Klamm didn't know him, just how to hunt him? Ask every little girl who lived within walking distance of the market if she knew Mr. Sam?

"I am," said Mendoza to himself, "going senile." He got up and went out to the anteroom. Sergeant Lake was smoking a cigarette with an air of martyrdom. Lake had never been a smoker, but he'd been putting on weight lately and had read somewhere that people who stopped smoking usually gained; he was trying an experiment in reverse. "Jimmy," said Mendoza, "I am not thinking straight. Who's here?"

"Nobody. There's still twenty-odd of these deviates to find."

"Yes. And let us, to maybe narrow it down some," said Mendoza, "look at the descriptions and see if any of them has red hair."

"My good God," said Lake mildly. "I don't think anybody thought of that one. Let us indeed. I've got the pedigrees here."

"Give, give," said Mendoza, and took them back to his desk.

Mrs. Adelbert Sorenson looked at Piggott and Glasser with horrified eyes. "Murdered!" she said. "*Raped* and murdered! An eight-year-old! Oh, my dear heaven, if we'd known—but we didn't! None of us did. Oh, my dear heaven—*it must have been that little girl!* It must have been—"

"You think you saw her?" asked Piggott.

She nodded vigorously.

They had just been thorough, checking back. They exchanged a glance, surprised and incredulous. It was eleven days ago, Marla forgetting her schoolbook, going to get it. Coming back from the Fosters' along Montana Street, turning at this corner. Where the old house made into a duplex stood.

"My dear heaven," she said. She was about forty-five, a little too plump, good-natured looking, ash-blond hair turning gray; she had on a neat pink cotton housedress with an apron over it. "It was that day. That you said. A week ago last Thursday. It *was*. You can ask Lorena, she'll back me up. Oh, my goodness. If we'd *heard* about it—but we never. We only got back this morning. Only reason we aren't to church—we only got back about half-past eleven. And that's the reason I can place it, you see. Oh, my dear Lord, that poor child. Eight years old, you said—Yes, she'd have been about that."

"You *saw* her, Mrs. Sorenson?" asked Glasser. "You're sure it was that day, a week ago Thursday? What time?" She couldn't possibly be sure.

"You can ask Lorena. My oldest daughter. She saw her too. We said then—Yes, I'm sure," she said. "Because it was just before the telegram came. Not fifteen minutes before. A nice sunny morning, those few nice days we had"—she glanced out at the rain—"and we were sitting on the porch. Lorena's nineteen, out of school, she's going to a secretarial school and her first class is at nine-thirty. She was just saying best she get ready to leave when we saw the little girl. School'd started, she was maybe late for some reason—along the street there, just across. Then this car stopped and she went and got in it. What? Why, no, she just went out into the street and got into the car, nobody tried to—my dear goodness, if we'd seen anybody *force* her into a car we'd have called the police quick, but it wasn't like that. I remember all right, you ask Lorena, I said, just making talk like, little girl late for school, it was maybe around eight-forty-five—and maybe got a lift from her daddy or somebody she knows. And it wasn't ten, fifteen minutes later when the wire came—about Bert's father dying. And I always say a blessing to go quick, heart attack it was, but hard on them that's left. And we had to pack in a hurry and drive up there, Bert the only child, and of course—him being a widower—we had to stay and sort things out, what to save and give away, and it was quite a job. We sent the children back with Lorena, stay with my sister, they're just up on Melbourne, so's they could go to school, but Bert and I had to stay on. And so we never *heard*. About the poor child getting murdered. Like that. We left about ten-thirty, all in a hurry, that same morning. If we'd *heard* about it, if we'd been home, Lorena and I'd have remembered—you can ask her— and told you people. Because you said right here, around here she'd have been going back to school—"

"Mrs. Sorenson," said Piggott, "you say you saw the little girl—and you remembered she had on a light-blue dress— get into a car. Of her own volition, not coerced—"

"*Or* we'd have called the police—"

"Yes. At about eight-forty-five, a week ago Thursday morning. You're sure?"

"I'm sure. You can ask Lorena."

"Can you give us any kind of idea what kind of car it was?"

And she said at once, definitely, "Why, yes. Some. It was an old gray sedan, I couldn't say the make, only saw it from behind, it was pointed down Montana across there, a middle-sized car, old but a sedan all right. And gray."

Piggott looked at Glasser. What Jason Grace had got from Greta— "You're sure, Mrs. Sorenson?"

"I'm positive. You can ask—"

Chapter Eleven

"Two?" said Hackett in surprise. He had just looked in to say that the latest one from records was definitely N.G., in time to hear what Piggott and Glasser had turned up.

"Don't be ridiculous, Art," said Mendoza. "I refuse to believe in two child-rapists picking two eight-year-olds from the same school within a week of each other. We know it's the same boy. Obviously, what this says—if both Mrs. Sorenson and Greta Larsen are right—is that he has access to both a sedan and a pickup truck."

"Well, I don't know," said Piggott. "A lot of people do have both, but not right around that neighborhood. Not a wealthy neighborhood."

"What says he comes from there?" asked Glasser. "He could live in Beverly Hills."

"One thing—he doesn't seem to have a job, wandering around like—"

"The one answers the other," said Mendoza, "doesn't it? Marla, eight-thirty or so—he was on his way to work. And Alice at twelve noon, he was on his lunch hour. And that says, doesn't it, he works around here somewhere."

"That makes sense, in a way," agreed Hackett.

"And access to doesn't say he owns both the sedan and the pickup. And be that as it may," said Mendoza, "I have come across exactly one red-haired man in these pedigrees.

I think we'd better find him and talk to him. Daniel O'Hanlon, last known address Fifteenth Street. And why didn't anybody but me think of connecting the records and the red hair?"

"Obviously because you're smarter," said Hackett. Palliser looked in the door.

"Conference? Look, this Streeter woman. She could have gone anywhere. Nobody knows anything. There's nowhere else to look. Let's throw it in Pending."

Mendoza of the tidy mind did not like throwing cases in Pending. "Where did she work? She had a job?"

"Sure. Same place that Doris Graham works. Same place Jeanie worked before she married Streeter. Cocktail waitress, place out on Vermont. I've been there—it's open twenty-four hours a day. Nobody knows anything," said Palliser, "and I don't think they're lying. Bell's in the clear. Jeanie just fixed up the job herself and, seeing that she'd had an abortion before—so she told Bell—it could be she went to the same place. If it's still operating. But there's no lead on it at all."

Mendoza admitted there didn't seem to be. "I wonder," he said suddenly, "if Marla knew Alice? The same age—same school. Same teacher."

"Well, they weren't best pals, we know that," said Hackett. "What does it matter?"

"It doesn't, I suppose. We know they'd both run into the red-haired man. And, I wonder, how many other little girls, on errands up to those stores?"

There was a moment of silence. Hackett got up. "What's the address on O'Hanlon? I'll see if I find him home—just time before lunch." He straightened his tie and went out.

"I suppose I'd better bring the report on Jeanie up to date," said Palliser morosely, and wandered out.

"It's funny," said Piggott. "The two cars. If they're both right."

"That Mrs. Sorenson sounded pretty positive," said Glasser.

"What's funny?" said Landers, coming in to hear that. "I just found another one, if anybody'd like to sit in on the questioning. What's funny?"

Piggott told him. Landers considered, boyish face thoughtful, and said, "I don't see it's so peculiar, Matt. When he picked up Marla he was in his own car—on the way to work. When he picked up Alice he was driving a pickup that belongs to where he works."

Mendoza sat up. "And that is an idea. I think you may have something there, Tom. That could be. But Greta didn't remember any sign on the pickup."

"Needn't have been one. Or she didn't notice."

"True. That is indeed a thought," said Mendoza, and Higgins came in. Piggott said they had a couple more to look at before lunch; he and Glasser went out.

"I had an idea," said Higgins, "about finding Red Hair. If he is a regular customer there, it could be that some of the other regular customers would know him, Luis. By sight. Maybe even know where he lives, or the general area. Nobody knows when this Klamm might get back, and we haven't any guarantee he knows him. I just thought—"

Mendoza opened his mouth to reply, and Sergeant Lake burst in.

"Traffic just called—at least one D.O.A. over on Sunset Place, a sniper loose—got a squad car pinned down—intersection of Seventh—"

All three of them sprang up. Mendoza swept open the top desk drawer and scooped up the gun and a box of ammo, snatched his hat, and followed Higgins and Landers out. In the lot downstairs, they fell into the Ferrari; the twelve-cylinder engine roared. "If I don't have a siren put on this thing before I'm—"

Fifteen minutes later, across a mile of town, they came on a besieged block. Unpretentious little homes along here, but on a Sunday noon a lot of people were home. There was a squad car at this end of the block; both uniformed men were squatted beside it, guns out, peering cautiously over the hood. There was an ambulance in the middle of the street, and a body lying in front of it: the body of a man. One of the interns from the ambulance had evidently been hit; he was lying in the street there, the other one giving him first aid. There was another body on the front lawn of the house directly across

from the squad car. And the citizenry were out in gabbling
curiosity, gawking and chattering and scattering as new shots
sounded. Another squad car was drawn up on the side street
here, and two harassed men from it were trying to protect the
citizenry. "Get in the house, ma'am, you'll be safer in—please,
sir, just go home, get under cover—take those children inside—"

A fusillade of shots from the house across the street. A
woman in a fur jacket over a long housecoat, standing on the
lawn next to the squad car, screamed and fell. One of the uniformed men hurried to her, crouching, and got her into the
shelter of the ambulance out there.

The men from Homicide left the Ferrari in the street and
ran over behind the first squad car. "What goes on?" asked
Higgins. "Drunk?"

"Your guess good as mine," said the uniformed man there,
his eyes on the house. "We get the call, a woman shot. We
come over. Sure enough—that one over there on the lawn. Cold.
This guy with a rifle there. Seemed dazed. I'm just about to take
the gun away, he's saying but he didn't mean to shoot *her,*
he was aiming for Clara, when be damned, he turns and runs
in the house and starts shooting. I think that guy out there is
dead. He was just walking by. If we could get a look at him,
even what room he's in over there—"

Another fusillade of shots. More screams. And a sudden
silence. In the middle of it, they heard the woman out there by
the ambulance, incoherent and shocked, as the intern worked
over her—"Just a flesh wound, you'll be O.K., ma'am," he was
saying. "Take it easy. Johnny, you all right? You're not bad,
it's just—"

"—*shot* her! Shot her, just like—It was Clara he wanted to
kill, he must be crazy, I never trusted him—told him she was
goin' to divorce him, couldn't stand his temper—he belted her
around some, I know—and she—and Clara just out there, yard
next door, cutting roses—Must be crazy! What're you *doin'* to
me? Oh, my God—"

"Gone berserk," said Higgins. "Damn, how much ammo has
he got in there?" Bullets sprayed wildly from the house.

"It's the right front window," said the squad-car man suddenly. It had stopped raining about half an hour before, the sun had come out, and the old-fashioned casement windows of the house were open, in front. The rifle had wreaked havoc on the screen. The squad-car man snapped off four quick shots, all of them through the screen, and immediately a barrage of rifle shots answered, most of them hitting the squad car. The other uniformed men had by now largely succeeded in herding the citizenry out of range.

"Nice quiet Sunday up to now," said the squad-car man conversationally. He fired two more shots and started to reload his gun.

The screen door over there opened, and a man came out onto the front porch. He wasn't a very big man; he had on a white shirt and dark pants, and he held his rifle with both hands. He fired at the ambulance. Then he turned the rifle quickly as the men behind the squad car got up, guns out ready. As he fired again, both Higgins and Landers fired almost simultaneously. Landers yelled and spun around and dropped heavily. Across the street the man with the rifle let go of it, bent double, and slid down quietly on top of it.

"Tom—" panted Higgins, turning Landers over. The intern came to them, running. The sudden silence after all the shots was shocking.

"Shoulder," said the intern, tearing open Landers' shirt. "Nasty, though—went through some muscle. He probably cracked his head falling. Is it all over? My God, when he started firing and got Johnny—"

Higgins and Mendoza went across the street. The man with the rifle was lying quietly on the porch. When they turned him over, they saw that one bullet had struck square over the heart.

"I wonder if it was Tom or me," said Higgins academically.

"Ballistics will be looking at both your guns to find out, George. For the formal hearing. Justifiable homicide," said Mendoza. "So let's sort out how many people he killed."

It turned out to be only the passerby and the woman on the lawn, but of course the paperwork on it would be something, all the statements. The wife, Clara, who was the cause of all this, was hysterical, and another ambulance was called.

Higgins went along with Landers in the first one, while Mendoza got names and addresses from all the witnesses.

It was two-thirty before Higgins came in to Federico's and joined Mendoza over a belated lunch. "Tom'll be O.K., they say. Slight concussion, and the bullet. About a week in. Thank God. Of all the senseless random things—Who was he, by the way?"

"One Chauncey Chalmers," said Mendoza, swallowing rye. "Annoyed because his wife was going to divorce him. She won't have to now. People. You're to turn your gun in to Ballistics."

"I've got Tom's too. He hadn't come to when I left, but they said he'd be O.K. People indeed. What made us want to be cops, Luis? Anyway?"

"Fellow I know," said Mendoza, "*and* a former good cop too, says it's built-in. Like with sheepdogs. Sheepdogs," he added to himself. "*Caray,* that's funny when you come to think of it."

Palliser, having brought the report on Jean Streeter up to date, went out for a solitary lunch. Sergeant Lake was on the phone as he passed, so he didn't hear about the sniper at all. He came back at one-thirty, and as he came up to the rank of elevators there was another man waiting there. Lieutenant Andrews of Vice. They greeted each other casually, the elevator came, and they got in. Palliser politely pushed the button for Andrews' floor, which came before Homicide.

"They keeping you busy?" asked Andrews.

"Brother," said Palliser, "you have said it." It occurred to him wistfully that if Jean Streeter hadn't happened to die of her botched lock-picking job, she would be Andrews' business right now and not his. Funny, wherever she'd gone, she'd expected—

The elevator landed, and as the door began to roll back, Palliser's mind jumped precisely from cause to effect. "Oh, Lieutenant," he said. "Did your boys just happen to drop on a lock-picking setup on Friday night?"

Andrews stopped halfway through the door and turned.

"Psychics we've got in Homicide? Besides our Luis? How'd you know?"

"By God, I'll bet that's it!" said Palliser. "I'll just bet! She'd fixed it up herself—and somebody picked her up about seven, took her there, and the butcher did the job—she expected to stay over Sunday, sure, only then you come staging the raid, and maybe she's the only patient on the premises, they bundle her out—oh, by God, yes!"

"What are you talking about?" asked Andrews.

"I want to hear about it. Where was it, the butcher's place?"

"You think it ties into something of yours? It was Rosabell Street, a little alley up from the main post-office. We got the tip—Well, if you want to see the records, come on." They got out of the elevator and started for Andrews' office. "We got the tip from the mother of a girl who'd gone there. Nearly died of septicemia, but pulled through O.K. and gave us the name. What's it tie up with?"

"By God, I'll bet," said Palliser. "They bundled her out quick, evidence against them, damn what state she was in, and she managed to get to the nearest public place open that time of night—Union Station. But nobody around to ask for help, and it could be she didn't realize she was as bad as she was, thought —Yes, the rest room, and she started hemorrhaging, and—"

"One of your bodies," said Andrews. "We landed there about midnight."

"Which also ties in," said Palliser. "I like it. The logical thing to do is see if any of Jeanie's fingerprints show up in the place. If they do, Q.E.D."

"Well, so let's hear the whole story. Sit down," said Andrews.

Hackett came in with Daniel O'Hanlon at three o'clock. He'd found the address all right, O'Hanlon still lived there, but he was out; the landlady, eyeing him suspiciously, had told him Danny'd be sure to be in at two-thirty, on account he never missed this program on television, a cartoon, he was crazy about cartoons. Which should have prepared Hackett for Danny.

Mendoza and Higgins had just come in, and Hackett heard

about the little party over on Sunset Place for the first time. "Little vacation for Tom," said Higgins. "Not that I envy him."

"What a thing," said Hackett. "He was lucky. You all were. I'll go see him—take him something to read, when he's sitting up. He likes science-fiction, I don't know why."

Daniel O'Hanlon, the one red-haired man in Records, they started to question with interest, but the interest soon waned. The record said the expectable things, indecent exposure, theft of underwear, solicitation of minors; he was thirty-two and had spent a total of seventeen months in jail. But O'Hanlon himself—

"Hey, I ain't done a thing," he told them genially. "Honest. That judge he said—last time I was up—about goin' to a head-doctor, and I done it. Thing they call a clinic at the General Hospital. A real nice guy, this head-doctor was, and he got me all straightened out and I don't want to do those things no more. Oh, well, just now 'n' then I get a kind of urge—but I ain't done nothing. Since. And I got a full-time job, work for the city, street gang on sewers an' like such, I been workin' full time—"

They got the name of his immediate boss and tried to check that, but on Sunday, of course, it was impossible.

"But," said Mendoza, "I really don't see O'Hanlon doing the magic tricks and charming little girls. Do you?"

Both Higgins and Hackett admitted that it took a lot of imagination. And O'Hanlon didn't live anywhere near that shopping section along Glendale. If Mr. Sam, hanging around there, was the boy they wanted, it looked doubtful that he was also Daniel O'Hanlon.

"Let him loose, and check out the alibi tomorrow," said Mendoza. "Just in case." Higgins and Hackett agreed. "Damn, I like this thing about Mr. Sam. If there was any way to—"

"What I said, other customers there," said Higgins tiredly, rubbing the back of his neck.

"And how do we find them?" asked Mendoza. "Klamm operates strictly on a cash basis—no credit. No names. Hang around the damn market and ask everybody who comes in? Damnation."

"Lieutenant," said Lake, looking in. "Jase on the phone."

"Let him go," said Mendoza, waving at O'Hanlon, and went into his office and picked up the phone. "Jase?"

"I'm interested in this red-haired fellow," said Grace's soft voice, "and it occurred to me—you know what a simple mind I've got—to wonder if anybody had checked where Klamm lives. I just did. *Via* the phone book. He'd got a house over on Rosemont Avenue. Married, but his wife's with him. The neighbors had heard about his legacy and going to San Francisco and all—nobody knows where he's staying there, no—but one fellow who seems to know him pretty well says he intended to be back by Tuesday."

"Well, praise heaven for small favors," said Mendoza. "Thanks very much."

"Mr. Sam," said Grace thoughtfully, "looks pretty hot to me."

"Very much a front-runner," said Mendoza. "Thanks, Jase."

And then Palliser came in, triumphant, with his hunch on Jeanie. Which looked very possible indeed.

"Andrews said by all they've got, this particular setup hasn't been going more than a year or so, so it probably wasn't the same place Jeanie went before. But however she heard about it, this is the answer—has to be. If her prints show up there—"

"It must be contagious, getting hunches," said Higgins. "You and the mastermind here."

"I wish to God I had a valid hunch on Marla and Alice," said Mendoza irritably. "What I have got is nothing. If we can ever locate Mr. Sam—"

"Haven't you got any further on it?" asked Angel, adding a dash of pepper to whatever was in the pan on the stove.

"One hot lead," said Hackett. Sheila staggered toward him on uncertain legs and he picked her up. "How's my Sheila-girl?" They had to catch this one, because so many little girls —innocent little girls—He hugged Sheila harder and she squealed.

"Dinner in fifteen minutes," said Angel. "You'll get him,

darling. . . . And it *is* the queerest thing about that dog. Alison phoned a while ago—"

"The shaggy dog." Hackett grinned. For Luis's sins. Casually, because he knew she'd see it in the papers, he told her about Landers.

Mendoza came home to be confronted with the spectacle of Sheba chewing diligently on one of Cedric's long ears while her mother washed his whiskers maternally. "I tell you what it is," said Alison. "These opportunists simply see he can be *used*. I can see it in Bast's eye. More food around to appropriate, and he doesn't mind washing them when they're feeling lazy."

"Slandering my cats like that," said Mendoza, "I will not—that lummox of a dog—"

"Really a very handsome dog," said Alison. "Hadn't you noticed how Máiri's cleaned him up?"

"That long coat, it needs taking care of," said Mrs. Mac-Taggart noncommittally. "And the beastie's so grateful for any attention."

Cedric indeed had been spruced up. His white chest, legs, and feet were chalky-white, combed out snowily, and his blue-gray parts shined up with a brush. His white whiskers were being polished by Bast, while Sheba rapidly undid all the work done on his long feathered ears. Nothing could be seen of his expression, but his pink tongue was out for an occasional affectionate slurp at one or the other of the cats.

"Up to now, quite intelligent cats," said Mendoza. *"Nobody's* called?"

"Nobody," said Alison. "I really don't think anybody will, now, Luis. Luis—"

"I read your mind," said Mendoza. *"¡Absolutamente no!"*

"Amante, the twins are—and he's so good with them—you know the cats never let themselves be played with much—"

"Having," said Mendoza, "some self-respect. Large shaggy dogs I have no especial affection for."

Alison exchanged a glance with Mrs. MacTaggart, who made a Scottish noise and vanished into the kitchen. Mendoza went to see the twins; Alison put dinner on the table, and when he

sat down, asked dutifully about his day, about the cases on
hand. "Nothing on the little girls? You've got to get that one,
Luis—"

"We will. One lead I like very much." He told her about it.

In the living room, he tried to put the cases out of his mind,
El Señor curled on his lap, *The Day's Work* open on top of El
Señor, the house silent around him: but his mind kept drifting
back to the red-haired man. Klamm home on Tuesday, to be
hoped: to be asked. Would he know? The best lead they had
really—That had been a very valid hunch of Palliser's. It would
probably turn out that that was where Jeanie had been. So,
Percy Andrews' case against the lock-picking setup handed
over to Homicide, and all the paperwork, *condenación*. . . .

El Señor hissed like a rattlesnake and left him abruptly. A
large round shaggy something pressed up under his hand,
which was hanging over the chair arm. Mendoza opened his
eyes.

"And who invited you in here?" he asked. He was alone in
the living room: Alison was busy over letters in the den
supposed to be his.

Cedric laid his head on Mendoza's knee and sneezed to show
his wall-eye. "You were not," said Mendoza, "invited here,
you know, *bufón*."

Cedric offered him a paw.

Mendoza roughed the hairy round head. "Is that what happened, *pobrecito?* They went off and left you, maybe you cost
too much to feed? Making up to my cats—an idiot clown of a
dog—and you know something, *bufón?*" Cedric put the other
front paw on his knee, listening. "I have the definite suspicion
that you're the kind of dog, the burglar shows up some night,
you'd welcome him in and lead him to the safe. You are a
fraud and a fawner." Cedric heaved his forequarters into
Mendoza's lap and aimed a slurp at Mendoza's mustache. "You
ought to learn from the cats, *bufón*. They don't love indis-
criminately. You're an incurable optimist, *¿cómo no?*" Cedric
washed his hand. "Was that it, *chasquear?* They left you, and
you're holding no grudge on people even so? The cats are
smarter." Cedric uttered a small sound and laid his head on

Mendoza's stomach. He was heavy and warm. Mendoza stroked his head.

"Well!" said Alison at the door. "What a touching sight. Master and dog."

"Will you kindly," said Mendoza, "get this creature off me? Everybody knows I am not a dog-lover. I'm sorry for the idiotic thing, I would not send it to the damn pound, but that does not say I want it in my lap."

"No, darling," said Alison. "Come, Cedric. Come to bed and leave master alone."

"And I am not his—"

Monday morning, and Piggott off. The routine yet to be done, fifteen men from Records still to find. And if Mendoza had a hunch, it was a hunch that that was wasted effort: their boy wasn't going to show there.

At nine o'clock he was demanded on the phone by Sergeant Barth, a Barth furious and raging. "That bastard—I *told* you, Lieutenant!—that bastard Nugent! He's got some damn smart-alec shyster, he's reneged on the confession, we browbeat it out of him when he was sick—and you know the damn-fool judges, who knows but what—?"

"*¡Carape!* You heard me warn him—"

"Yes, yes, but these brutal sadistic cops always stick to-gether, didn't you know? A deputy D.A. just called me—I *told* you," said Barth. "Sick! He had one hell of a hangover, and—"

"Well, it's not the first time it's happened," said Mendoza. "Annoying, but—"

"I know, I know. And that female, Louella what's-her-name, seemed like a reasonably honest woman, she'll probably testify to the hangover—unless the lawyer gets to her first—"

"Reasonably." Mendoza laughed. "Hadn't laid eyes on him till two days before. Checked into a motel with him—"

"I said reasonably. But, damn it—"

"So he might get off with manslaughter. We can prove he owns the Pontiac, but he can always claim he loaned it to a friend a day or two before—and, depending on the judge—Our job," said Mendoza, "is just to catch them, Barth. So I'll see you at the inquest. We'll see what transpires."

"These Goddamn—" said Barth. "All right. I'll see you."

It was, of course, annoying. Frustrating.

Higgins came in and said this new one looked a little funny. The landlady had called in, just as the shift was changing. One of her roomers dead. San Julian Place. "The interns said it looks like a heart attack, a stroke—natural, anyway—but he was a bum, Luis—seven-dollar-a-week room, the old clothes from the Salvation Army, the empty bottle of sauterne in a corner, a bum, a lush. Only in a drawer in the dresser, a thousand bucks in cash. All in twenties. Funny."

"Funny," said Mendoza. "Yes. If it was a natural death, nothing for us to follow up, George. Windfall for the state."

"I suppose," said Higgins, and wandered out. Hackett came in and said that O'Hanlon's alibi had checked out. He'd been on the job, the city job, full time last Friday and all the week before.

"Una sorpreesa no es," said Mendoza. "Red hair or no, he didn't look likely. Red hair. I do wish—Klamm. But would he—?"

Sergeant Lake looked in. "The principal of that school's on the phone. That little girl's sweater just turned up. Alice Stark's. Just now. Her name in it. In the schoolyard. He thought you'd like to know."

Chapter Twelve

"DAMNATION," said Mendoza, "I've got to get to that inquest. You chase over to the school, see if it's a lead." He snatched up his hat and fled.

And the white cardigan said a little something, but not much. Hackett and Higgins found the principal waiting for them with a serious, bespectacled eleven-year-old who had found the sweater. Who was only one of a dozen kids who could swear it hadn't been there on Friday—just behind the baseball diamond, hanging on the fence. They let him show them exactly where—"I had to shin up the fence to get it down, and when I saw the name in it I took it to Mis' Collison, and she—"

About six feet up, hanging on an outward-turned bit of the chain-link fence, on the inside. "So," said Higgins, turning it over in his big hands, "she left it in the pickup, and he didn't notice it until after he'd got away from the park. He got rid of it here. Tossed it over the schoolyard fence, thinking if it's found here we'll just think she left it here. Forgot it."

"Yes," said Hackett. He took the sweater and looked at the name-tag inside the collar. No need to bother the Starks; the name-tag had been there a while. The sweater was dirty, and Hackett doubted that it had been this dirty when Alice started for school on Friday morning. "And it is a high fence, and the gates are locked over the weekend, I think. Maybe he weighted it with something—" there were loose rocks around on the packed dirt of the playground, this near the fence—"to get it over, and then it caught there, falling—where she couldn't possibly have put it. Anyway, George, it won't do any harm to let the lab see it." The lab had come up with nothing useful on either Marla's or Alice's clothes so far, but—

They thanked the principal, and delivered the sweater to the lab. Glasser had brought in another man from Records, so they sat in on that and got nothing but a tentative alibi.

At eleven-twenty Mendoza came back, looking irritated, and said this and that about that smart-alec lawyer of Nugent's. "More of the police brutality bit. We were mean to him, and bullied him into confessing when he never done it at all, honest to God it was two other guys. He was just scared of the big sadistic cops."

"Did the bench listen?" asked Hackett.

"It was only an inquest. He looked bored. What he didn't say, hash it over at the trial. The D.A.'s deputy had evidence after all—the car belongs to Nugent, the blonde could say he'd been driving it around for at least two days before, and the body only got in the trunk on that Monday night. They held him on homicide-first, no bail. Which is something."

"At least," agreed Higgins. They told him about the sweater and he shrugged.

"Unless the lab gets something interesting from it, it takes us no further." And then Sergeant Lake came in and said Miss Sutcliffe and Dr. Clifford were here and would like to see him. "Oh, hell," said Mendoza. "To ask how come Nugent's saying, not guilty, when I told them it was all tied up. And I can't tell them he mightn't get off, either. Depending on what kind of jury he gets. All right, shove them in, Jimmy." He lit another cigarette.

Hackett and Higgins went out past them, and got back to the routine. There were still a lot of statements to get from yesterday's little shooting-party witnesses; they started to get this cleared up, with Glasser and Grace.

Mendoza got rid of Anita Sutcliffe and Clifford, after explaining some of the facts of life to them, at about noon. He was still having the vague hunch that the routine was not going to turn up their boy, but he hadn't as yet any hunch as to what might. All he knew was that he wanted to locate that Mr. Sam, as the hottest lead they had; and he went out for the Ferrari and drove up there to that little block of shopping section on Glendale Avenue.

He didn't go into the market; Barlow was no help. He tried the hardware store, and the owner and one clerk were eager to be helpful but couldn't offer him anything. "Red hair? Well, now, Mr. Fletcher has kind of auburn hair—would you say, Bill?— he might be the one—though, my goodness, a nice old man and I can't think the *police* would be asking—excuse me, what *is* it about?—well, excuse me, I know you don't go round telling everything about—Red hair, you call anybody else to mind, Bill?" Bill didn't. Temporarily discounting old Mr. Fletcher as a possible candidate for Mr. Sam, Mendoza tried the drugstore. The pharmacist, a middle-aged man with brisk manners, was more on the ball.

"*Red* hair," he said. "Real red hair, sir? Well, there is a man like that comes in here once in a while—not very often. I don't know his name. Just, maybe, six-seven times the last, oh, year. A man, late thirties maybe, buys shaving cream, razor blades, paperback books—but he's not what I'd call a regular customer. Don't recall that he's been in for a couple of months. Sorry, sir." He looked interested, but didn't ask questions.

So, thought Mendoza, stake the place out until Mr. Sam came in again? *¡Mil rayos!* And with Landers on the sick list—

He went up to Federico's for lunch and met Hackett and Higgins at the door.

"That thing still bugs me, Luis," said Higgins. "The old bum with the grand in cash. I know, probably nothing to do with us, it looked like a natural death, but it's funny."

"We've got enough to do without worrying about things that aren't our business," said Hackett. "I'll indulge myself with the steak sandwich and French-fried onions, I was down three pounds this morning."

"Congratulations," said Mendoza absently. "I suppose we

could brief that druggist to—But how could he get the name? Short of picking his pocket—¡*Condenacion!*"

"What?" said Hackett.

"Bring me the steak sandwich. . . . *Nada*," said Mendoza. "I wish to hell—"

Palliser pulled up a chair and said to the waiter, "The small steak. Quick—I'm starved. Well, it proved out, so it's our baby now. That lock-picking pair. Jeanie's prints were all over a back room at that Rosabell Street place. So that's where she went for it. So now we go question the doctor and break him down to admitting it."

"Oh, hell," said Mendoza. "More paperwork. Why do you have to be so brilliant, John? What'd Percy have on it?"

"Just two of 'em. Elderly doctor—Norman Milton—struck off the register about twenty years back for the same thing—also, now, a lush. And a woman, Martha White, they thought was the business head, running Milton really. They're over in the Alameda facility, due for arraignment tomorrow."

"Which will now be postponed until we get further statements. And a new warrant on the homicide. Damn it, I just wish we got things one at a time occasionally," said Mendoza.

He went to see the doctor and his running mate with Hackett and Palliser after lunch. A uniformed jailer brought them into an interrogation room at that new, large jail—a stout old man in shabby stained clothes, bald head, flabby jowls, shaky hands, and bleary eyes; and a woman about fifty, a henna-haired brash-looking woman with hard blue eyes and a slit of a mouth undisguised by orange lipstick carefully outlining a new full mouth. She looked at them and said, "New set of cops." The old man just sat down wearily in the chair Hackett held for him.

"That's right, Miss White—is it Miss?"

"Good as anything else," she said shortly. "So what do you want?"

"We've just found that you—or rather the doctor—had a client last Friday evening. She expected to stay, and be looked after, until Sunday—after the job was done—but when the Vice cops started banging on the door, you bundled her out the back way, didn't you?" Her eyes narrowed, but she said nothing. "Though she wasn't in a very—mmh—capable condition to be under her own steam, was she? Out she went, as visible evidence, and you tried to get rid of all the other evidence in a hurry, we understand from Lieutenant Andrews—the instruments under the loose floorboard and the bloodstained towels in the garbage can—"

"I don't have to say anything to you," she said contemptuously.

The old man looked up vaguely. "But it wasn't right, Martha," he said. "It wasn't ethical. I always—a doctor ought to —responsible to his patients. Come—good faith—to a doctor. It wasn't right."

"You shut up, you old fool," she said sharply.

"You did do a job that night, didn't you, doctor?" asked Hackett.

He drew himself up slightly. "I *am* a doctor. They said— mustn't call myself—but I am. Yes. And it wasn't right." He looked at the woman. "Locks away the whisky," he muttered. "Until I've done—those jobs. She's a hard woman. Mersh— mercenary female. And I've—got—to—have—the whisky. Keep goin'. At all. But I said—it wasn't right."

"Listen, you old lush—"

"Doctor—" said Palliser gently, and unexpectedly the old man began to cry.

"They don' call me Doctor any more. The first time I ever —did that, ever—what should I do, what would I do? My own li'l girl. Poor li'l girl—only sixteen—an' I—But they found out. 'N' m' wife left me—accounta no more money."

"Oh, for God's sake!" said the woman. "You can see for yourself he don't know what he's talkin' about."

"Oh, doesn't he?" said Hackett. "It wasn't right to shove the woman out like that, just to try to save your own necks. Mrs. Jean Streeter—whether that was the name she gave you or not. It's a waste of time for you to go on denying it—we found her prints all over the back room of that house on Rosabell. She was there on Friday night—"

"God damn the bitch," said Martha White. "So she went and ratted to the law, did she? I didn't think that one would —all business, she was. Jean Smith. I'll be damned." She scowled at them.

"I don't think, Miss White," said Mendoza, "that you were introduced to us."

"Who needs introductions to fuzz? I'll be damned, that bitch—"

"We're from Homicide, Miss White. Mrs. Streeter didn't tell us about you, except—mmh—indirectly. She's dead, Miss White. She got as far as Union Station and bled to death. So you won't be up on a Vice charge. Accessory before and after to homicide, Miss White."

Her mouth opened and she stared at them, her throat working. "Dead? Hom——oh, my Christ! Oh, my God!" And she turned on Milton in fury. "Jesus God, I shoulda got shut of you—Dirty old lush doctor, forgot everything you ever knew —It was *him* did it, it was *him* used the knife, I didn't have anything to do with—"

"The law sees it a little different," said Hackett dryly. "You'll have time to think about it, Miss White. Would you like to make a statement?"

She swore at him obscenely. "No, I would not, cop!"

The old man was still crying.

"Well, anyway he's out of business," said Higgins on the way back to the office. "He'll probably get life and won't last a year without the whisky. Her, a different story." She could be out within five years.

Hackett went from the jail to see Landers in the General Hospital, stopping at a drugstore for a random selection of paperback books. He found Landers feeling very sorry for himself.

"Hell of a thing," he grumbled, "letting that idiot put me out of commission like this! My head aches and this shoulder's giving me hell and the damn nurse said I can't have another shot till—"

"Be thankful you're still here," said Hackett. "You could have been killed, Tom."

"By the damn fool running berserk." Landers growled. "So all right, count my blessings. I don't feel like it. And if you really want to be helpful, you can take my keys and go get me some pyjamas. These damn hospital gowns—I'm not used to going around in a mini-skirt, and in front of all these nurses yet—"

"All right, we'll see you get some. Cheer up," said Hackett. "You're getting a free vacation, Tom."

"Vacation, he says. If they'd let me go home—I've got a thing about hospitals. I don't like 'em. All these nurses calling me *we*. And I'm out of cigarettes. Look," said Landers, "when you go to get the pyjamas, Art, there's a bottle of bourbon in the cabinet over the sink—if you could smuggle it in—"

"I don't think the doctor—"

"Oh, damn the doctor," said Landers. "Letting myself get shot up—"

"At least it wasn't for nothing," said Hackett. "We got the word from Ballistics this morning, it was your gun killed him."

"Oh, he's dead?" said Landers with faint interest. "Well, good riddance. *My* gun. Oh, for God's sake, that means—"

"Well, yes, the formal hearing, but you know it's just the formality. Justifiable homicide. And when you were wounded—"

"The luck I've been having lately," said Landers, "I should go and shoot myself. Did you know I was out till midnight last night? This concussion. I didn't remember a thing from the time we left the office till, bang, I wake up here with an old bat bending over me saying she's the night nurse. Face to stop a—"

"But a very good nurse," said a cool voice behind Hackett. "Miss Fawcett. I hope you won't be complaining about me, Mr. Landers. I'm the afternoon nurse. The one you didn't remember, who took care of you when you came in."

Landers gaped at her. Hackett turned. She stood there, neat and trim, brown-haired and smiling, about twenty-five and very pretty, with a firm mouth and a stubborn-looking chin.

"Oh," said Landers weakly.

"After all, we have to take good care of our police," she said briskly, advancing on him. "Open your mouth—that's the way." She popped a thermometer in, and Landers looked helplessly at Hackett.

"I'll—er—bring you what you want, Tom," said Hackett, and retreated hastily. He hoped that strong-minded female didn't develop any designs on Landers: any man a babe in the woods against her.

Mendoza had just got back to the office at three o'clock, to find Hackett gossiping with Higgins about some nurse. He'd been down in Vice talking to Andrews about the case against the White woman. "Is this what you're paid for? God knows there's enough to do around here—" Sergeant Lake looked in and he uttered a groan. "Don't tell me, something new?"

"No, your outside phone," said Lake, looking a little excited. Mendoza sat down at the desk and picked it up.

"Mendoza, Homicide."

"Oh," said a man's voice. "Oh—*Homicide?* Well, I'll be damned. My name's Ralph Klamm. I just got home, and my clerk tells me there've been cops around wanting to talk to me. Well, I try to be a good citizen and any way I can help you fellows, but what *Homicide* might want with—Barlow just gave me the phone number you left—"

"Mr. Klamm. Where are you? We'll be right down—"

"Well, I'm at the store. Naturally. But what—?"

"*Bueno.* Stay there. We'll be with you in fifteen minutes." Mendoza slammed the phone down and reached for his hat. "Come on!" Their one hot lead might be about to break. Hackett and Higgins followed him out; a slow ride down in the elevator, and then Mendoza was gunning the Ferrari.

"He might not place him at all," said Higgins.

"And he might," said Hackett. "Only smell of a chance we've got—and if you ask me, once we find Mr. Sam we'll crack the case. He's the best possible that's showed up, considering what Sorenson and Greta said—"

"I'm just keeping my fingers crossed," said Higgins.

Mendoza braked the Ferrari in front of the market, and they went in. "Mr. Klamm? Lieutenant Mendoza. Sergeant Hackett, Sergeant Higgins. What we want to ask you—"

"Howdy-do," said Klamm. He was a big friendly-looking man with a lot of curly gray hair and an incipient paunch. "I don't know how I can help you, Barlow said about those two poor little girls, a terrible thing, makes you wonder what gets into people, but—"

"Mr. Klamm. Can you tell us anything about a man who may have come into your market a few times—or a lot of times—a man in his thirties, with red hair? His first name may be Sam. Does that—?"

Klamm stared at them. "This is about the two little—*Sam?* Why, you aren't going to tell me you mean Mr. DeVries? Mr. *DeVries?* Why, that's just impossible, gentlemen—on *that*. Mr. DeVries. His first name is Samuel, sure, I've cashed checks for him, but—What? Well, if it's Mr. DeVries you're talking about, which strikes me as just impossible, gentlemen—on a thing like that—sure, he stops in here all the time, he lives in an apartment over on Avalon, this is on his way home, and he— What? Why, he's got a photographic studio a couple of blocks up from here, DeVries' Art Studio—he took all the wedding pictures when my daughter got married last year, but on a thing like those two poor little—Gentlemen, it's impossible—"

They were already out of the market. He stared after them worriedly.

It was a small storefront, smart-looking, synthetic stone and a bay window. DeVries' Art Studio, said the sign, and in the bay window against an artistically draped velvet backdrop was a single portrait of a pretty dark-haired girl in evening dress. It was a very good photograph. A small sign in the front corner of the window said, Wedding Photographs, Studio Portraits, Family Groups, or your Favorite Pets—Come in and Discuss Arrangements.

They went in, and a little bell rang. A cheerful voice called instantly from somewhere beyond a curtained doorway, "Be with you in a minute!"

It was a tastefully arranged little anteroom, beige carpet, framed photographs on the walls, a small blond desk, a beige love seat and a pair of matching chairs.

"An *artiste*," said Higgins, "and they do so often go in for the sex deviation, don't they?"

"You can't generalize," said Hackett; and the curtain was pulled aside and their quarry entered. They knew him instantly. He was a thinnish, tallish man with a bush of fox-red hair, a long nose, and a wide mouth. He was wiry and lank, in a neat gray suit, white shirt, and silver tie, and he wore owlish horn-rimmed glasses. He looked a little surprised to find three men in his waiting room, two of them looming over him, and at the absorbed interest in their eyes.

"Well, what can I do for you?" he asked. "Sit down, won't you?"

"You can answer some questions," said Mendoza, producing his badge. "Mr. DeVries, is it? Did you ever get acquainted with some little girls, Mr. DeVries, over at Mr. Klamm's market —do the magic tricks for them, and maybe tell them little jokes? Did you tell them to call you Mr. Sam?" And they were all watching him.

DeVries stared at them. "Police—" he said; and then he said in naked utter astonishment, "You mean you think *I*— those two—Oh, my God. Oh, my dear God, if there was anything any human being could laugh at in that, it'd be—" He stopped. He said, "Yes, I knew those little girls. Little Alice —such a prim little thing, like my—like Mary. She always said *Mr*. Sam. If you want to know, I've talked to other kids I run into, too. There—other places. And you thought—" He shook his head. He went over and locked the front door, saying, "I haven't got an appointment until four." He stayed there, head bent, back to them, and said, "If you want to know. I've had masses said for them. I—I know they weren't Catholic, but —You—I suppose I'd better tell you."

"We'd like to hear anything you have to tell us, Mr. De-Vries," said Mendoza carefully, "but I have to inform you that you have a right to remain silent, and to have a lawyer present if you—"

DeVries made an impatient gesture. He turned and took off his glasses, and immediately his blue eyes took on the blind look of the myopic. He half-sat on the corner of the desk. "I like kids," he said. "That's all. Most of 'em have been all carefully warned about the strangers, and that's fine. Like we always warned—But they see I don't mean any harm, they'll talk to me—I do the little tricks, they always like that. Mary and Mike always liked—" he stopped and got out a clean handkerchief and began to polish his glasses. "It just makes it a little easier sometimes, to talk to the kids. Hear them giggle at the tricks. I—" he stopped again and then he said very quickly, "My —my wife and our two kids, they—it was a fire, at night, the trailer—they couldn't get out—trailer camp, it was when I was in the army. There wasn't time—Mary was seven and Mikie nine. And—Marge. Too. And I—just like once in a while to talk with the kids. Like that. Like they were—Mary and Mike." He gave them a blind twisted smile and put the handkerchief away. "Not—anything wrong, did you say Lieutenant? Not—that, I really do assure you. I suppose you've talked to the kids? The nice little girls. And heard about Sam with his magic tricks." He spread his hands: big square hands, very clean; and he shrugged. "And you wondered. I don't blame you. Looking for —one like that. My sweet Jesus Christ," and it was not profanity, "at least I know my Mary didn't die like that. . . . So you come asking. I don't blame you at all. I'm sorry you've wasted your time. It was just harmless old Samuel, acting maudlin over the kids because once, a while ago, he had a couple of his own. That's all."

And they didn't have to ask him for an alibi, where he'd been last Friday noon or a week ago Thursday morning. All they had to do was look at his eyes, naked without the disguise of the glasses. He was older than he looked, by ten years, maybe. All three of them had, at home, the hostages to fortune. If Higgins' hostages were Bert Dwyer's kids, well, Bert had been a friend of his and now they were his in a way too. And Hackett's heart gave a funny double thump and he thought, *Sheila*. And Mendoza had a sudden flashback to

Alison crossly demanding that he fasten her shoes—"It's all your fault I can't reach them myself—"

He said violently, "*¡Diez millones de demonios desde el infierno!* Damn you for a sentimental meddler, DeVries! You were our one hot lead—we really thought when we found you we'd have him! And you leave us with nothing, damn it—nowhere to go!"

DeVries put his glasses on slowly and his eyes swam back into focus. After a moment he said mildly, "No questions? No demands for alibis? Well. I can only say I'm sorry."

"You're not anywhere near as sorry as we are," said Hackett. "Now where *do* we go, Luis?" He sounded baffled.

"And I wish I could help you," said DeVries. "The two nice little girls. I think I'd give my life to help you get that one. But—" he smiled wryly "—it's easy to say, isn't it? All I can do is wish you luck. And offer up a few prayers. Which I will do."

They sat in Mendoza's office, where the three of them had wrestled with so many problems before, Mendoza chain-smoking. "You know, Luis," said Higgins hesitantly, "the Academy. The rookies. Up there. The first class is at nine and the lunch break twelve to one. If—"

"Do not recite absurdities to me, George," said Mendoza. "Before he's sworn in, every one of those men is screened as thoroughly as the F.B.I. could do it. Don't be ridiculous."

"It just occurred to me. I know it's almost impossible."

"There's just nowhere to go," said Hackett dismally. "The familiar stranger, all right—they got into the car, the pickup, willingly—if Sorenson and Greta are right. But who? Possibly? Tackle the parents again—try to build a list of the men they knew just casually—"

The inside phone rang on Mendoza's desk and he picked it up. "Mendoza . . . Yes? What? *¡Jesú, María, y José!* Now what does that say, for God's sake? All right, thanks so much. . . . Scarne." He put out his cigarette and lit another with a snap of the gold desk-lighter. "That sweater. Guess what they found on it. Besides miscellaneous dirt. Commercial-type furniture glue and a trace of turpentine. *¿Cómo les parece?*"

"What?" said Hackett. "Furniture glue—"

Grace came in and said he'd heard their hot lead had petered out. "Funny. He looked so—"

"Yes." Mendoza told him about the lab. "*Furniture* glue. Who uses that?" said Grace thoughtfully. "Carpenter, painter for the turpentine—"

"Rich man, poor man, beggarman, thief," said Mendoza sardonically. "Eeny meeny miny mo. I am fresh out of hunches."

"See the parents again," said Higgins stubbornly. "Ask about the familiar strangers. The ones like DeVries, but—and my God, would the parents *know?* If the mailman, the Helms Bakeries driver, had approached the kids somewhere else—"

"*De veras,*" said Mendoza.

"There are about thirty men out of Records," said Grace, "who are still possible. If—"

"He's not there," said Mendoza positively. "But we have to do the routine on it. So go look at them closer. Just for something to do."

"And you," said Hackett seriously, "had better have a hunch, Luis. Which direction to go."

"We can hope," said Mendoza. He sat there, smoking quickly, when they had gone out, and nothing at all occurred to him; his mind was blank of ideas. The discovery of Mr. Sam had produced a kind of catharsis in him, and his mind seemed to be taking a brief—it was to be hoped—holiday. He didn't see anywhere to go on this important one, the rape-killer of the two little girls. The one they had to get.

The outside telephone shrilled, a call automatically put through by Lake, and he picked it up. "Mendoza."

"Barth. I've been talking with that deputy D.A. He thinks we can prove it on Nugent in spite of the lawyer, with what we've got. I don't know. It's kind of up in the air. But what he said, I feel better about it anyway. I've got," said Barth, "an orderly mind. I don't like things up in the air. Uncertain."

"What we so often get," said Mendoza.

"Yeah. I hope we can nail Nugent. I'm a fool," said Barth, "to let things bother me. Grow an ulcer if I'm not careful. But

I can't help it. Things come along, they bug me. Like that damn dog. I had the woman on the phone again just now, and what the hell could I tell her? I mean—"

"Dog?" Mendoza had been doodling on his memo pad. He found he had drawn a proud hairy Cedric surrounded by four idiotically affectionate cats.

"Yeah," said Barth. "Damndest thing. Last week it was, a week ago Sunday night. Freeway crash—head-on. One of those things, up on the Hollywood freeway. The drunk crossing over into an oncoming lane—hit this out-of-state car head-on. A mess. Out-of-state car absolutely innocent, doing about thirty-five in the far-right lane. And a whole family wiped out —parents and two kids, seven and ten, my God. Drunk got a broken leg. You might know. But the crazy thing is—they were from a wide place in the road, Hays Fork, Indiana—the family —visiting his brother and sister-in-law here. And the sister-in-law—and the brother too of course—say they had this dog with them. A big dog. Some kind of sheepdog. And there's no sign of a dog at all, I tell you. Hurt or dead or whatever. The only reason she keeps after it, she says the dog is valuable. They paid a hundred bucks for him, she says. I ask you. Do I get paid to look for lost dogs, with all these pros—*and* amateurs —running loose? I ask you—"

"Oh," said Mendoza. "Oh. A sheepdog. I think maybe you'd better give me that name and address."

"What? Why? The damn dog—a Mrs. Ruggles, over in Huntington Park. Why?"

Mendoza added some feathery lines to Cedric's whiskers and said irritably, "The *address,* Barth."

Chapter Thirteen

"SO THAT," said Mendoza, "is where Cedric came from, *cara*. Now we know. Off the Hollywood freeway. After that crash."

"The poor darling," said Alison. "It's a mercy he wasn't killed—I don't see how he escaped at all."

"It was a convertible, Barth said. He was probably thrown out—and just lucky it wasn't in the way of traffic behind," said Mendoza. He looked at Cedric. Cedric the invader had achieved the living room; he was lying in the middle of it, happily, with Bast making bread on his chest and Sheba chewing left ear. Nefertite and El Señor were still being aloof, not because either of them had any illusions that Cedric was dangerous, but out of caution and contrariness.

"However," said Mendoza, "the fact remains that this woman—Mrs. Ruggles—is probably the legal owner. Or her husband. Relatives of the owners."

"Yes," said Alison, "but—"

"That's plain enough, isn't it?"

"I suppose so. The twins will be heartbroken, Luis. And, well, just by what you said this Sergeant Barth said, she—the woman—doesn't sound much—well, concerned about Cedric. Just—"

"That has nothing to do," said Mendoza, "with the legalities."

"Well, no," agreed Alison, looking at Cedric. "But he is such a darling clown—"

"Clown is the word," said Mendoza. He brushed his mustache the wrong way, and back again, looking at Cedric. "My otherwise sensible cats—a new plaything is all. New interest. If anybody had told me I'd see the day when Bast took up with a dog—"

"But not quite an ordinary dog, *querido,*" said Alison. "When you think, a very resourceful and intelligent dog—escaping from that awful crash, and getting all the way down into Hollywood safely—"

"And having the sense to pick your car out of the thousands available to him—the perennial sucker for any animal of whatever species," said Mendoza.

"Well, a lot of people would—" began Alison hotly, and stopped. "I suppose that is the law. This woman the nearest relative—or her husband."

"I suppose so," said Mendoza. "It's got to be the right dog —unusual circumstances. And here is the name and address. You'd better take him there tomorrow."

"Oh, dear," said Alison. "The twins—really, Luis—"

"Because, after all," said Mendoza, "police officers are supposed to uphold law and order. And—"

"Yes, I know. I'm only saying—oh, damn," said Alison. "The twins—"

"And we are supposed to raise our offspring in the same tradition."

"*Querido,* it is not so easy to explain abstruse rules of law to a two-and-a-half-year-old," said Alison. "All *right.*"

"And just tell the woman how it came about. All fortuitous."

"All right, I said I would."

Cedric beamed up at them happily, shaking his face-veil to show his eyes, the one brown and honest and friendly, the other blue-white and horribly crossed. He shook off Sheba momentarily and nearly knocked her over with a slurp of his tongue.

"After all, we've taken good care of him, and God knows

you tried to find out where he came from. All those ads. The cats will forget him in twenty-four hours, and the offspring—well, it's just as well to learn early in life that you can't have everything you want," said Mendoza sententiously.

"Yes," said Alison. "But what about *Cedric?* This woman—"

"Is the legal owner. Indubitably."

"Yes," said Alison, sounding dissatisfied.

"So you will see to it."

"While you are hard at work protecting the citizens. . . . *Nothing* more on that—?"

"No, damn it. Our one hot lead just dissolved—"

Tuesday morning, and Palliser's day off. Roberta had a list of a dozen houses to drag him through. But she was a model wife so far, and he indulged her.

The inquest on Alice Stark was scheduled for 10 A.M., and Mendoza would attend that. Meanwhile, the first call of the day came in just as the shift was changing, at eight o'clock: the squad car first to respond notified Homicide. The owner of a liquor store close in on Wilshire had come to open up, to find his night clerk dead on the floor and the cash register open.

Mendoza went over with Hackett to look at it. The owner was a Charles Everman and he was still in a little state of shock, talking compulsively.

"My God, Jim Seligman, as nice a fellow as I ever knew. Of all the rotten bad luck—my God, somebody'll have to see his wife and tell her—I always told him, you get the holdup, don't argue, hand over the money. But I guess Jim just wasn't built that way—an ex-Marine, you know, a very nice guy, and only fifty, my God. I come up to the door and find it open—that is, unlocked—and I come in and see him there, the gun—"

The lab truck was already there. Mendoza and Hackett had already noticed the gun. The dead man was lying prone between two sections of counter, as if he'd been on his way out from behind the counter, and the gun was a couple of feet ahead of his one extended arm.

"What about the gun, Mr. Everman? His?"

"It's *my* gun. That I always keep on the shelf under the register, see. I went and took that special course the National Rifle Association gives, in shooting for protection. What I tell my clerks is one thing, it's my business if I decide to stand up to the hood with a gun. But Jim didn't need any course—did I tell you he was an ex-Marine?—and he knew it was there. Loaded. I guess he just tried to take the guy, and—"

There were two bullets fired from Everman's gun, which was a Colt .38. And presently the lab men came on some patches of what looked like blood, on the floor near the front door.

"Maybe Jim winged him, by God!" said Everman. "These goddamn hoods—killing as nicea guy as—"

Maybe he had indeed, and just in case they sent out the usual notice to hospitals and clinics, to watch for the possible gunshot wound. The lab men were also finding a fine collection of latent prints all over the counter, both sections of it near the body, and on the register, and elsewhere. It would be a well-patronized store, on a main drag. And whether any of the prints belonged to the holdup man they might in time find out; it was unlikely, of course. They took the corpse's prints as a check. Mendoza and Hackett questioned Everman patiently, trying to pin down times.

"He came on duty at six, that's right, worked here nearly five years since he got retired from the Marines—six to midnight, we're open till midnight, and he was on all day Saturdays and Sundays—we're open seven days a week—I left about six-ten last night—yes, he'd lock up, you don't need a key to do that—switch on the burglar alarm and all—and then I opened up at eight. Just like today, I come up and see the door isn't locked, and I—"

The interns said provisionally, eleven to midnight last night, and it looked like a big gun; he'd been shot twice. Not surprising that nobody had heard the shots: this was the only store in this block open after six at night.

The inquisitive lab men were now out in the street, and presently Scarne came back looking pleased and said they'd found a big gob of blood up there about fifteen feet from the front door, right at the curb. "Where he was parked, maybe? Could be he was hit pretty bad."

"Could be," agreed Hackett. "If so—"

"And we got some beautiful latents off the register there— the side of it. Fresh as daisies," said Scarne. "I'll give 'em a quick run-through in the cross-file. Just maybe we'll get a break on this one."

"I'm taking no bets," said Hackett.

Mendoza left him there taking notes and went back to the office to see if anything else had come in. There was another body, looked like a suicide from the first report; Piggott had gone out on it with Higgins. There were still a few statements to get on Chalmers; Grace was out on that with Glasser.

And at ten, this inquest. And this afternoon, Alice Stark's funeral.

Mendoza was taking no bets that something else wouldn't come up. The something else so often did.

When Hackett got back to the office to type up the report on Jim Seligman, everybody else was out. He pulled his tie loose and started the report, but his mind wouldn't stay on it, even on the automatic typing, and he began to make mistakes, and swore, and x-ed out a whole line.

If it wasn't one thing it was seven, he thought. Jumping from one job to another, back and forth, and trying to keep everything straight on every single damned case—and they weren't supermen, after all, but everyday human beings. A *little lower than the angels,* said his mind. He amended to that, said it twice. A lot of the people they ran into were one hell of a lot lower.

"Provisional time of death 11-12 P.M., February 49th," he typed, and swore and x-ed out the figures. The 49th of February, now there was a day for you, and if he didn't put his mind on the job—

DeVries. Oh, that poor damned devil DeVries. Such a hot lead he had looked. And fizzling out like that. Where could they look now, on this one they had to get, the killer of the innocents?

The familiar strangers. Try to pry some names out of the parents, the men the little girls had known? If just known. Men coming to the house on lawful occasions—

He thought suddenly, but they had both known him. That, they knew, didn't they? As per Sorenson and Greta. To both the little girls he had been the familiar stranger.

Some vague idea was floating around at the back of his mind, and he abandoned the report to let it float closer. He sat back, lit a cigarette, and shut his eyes.

Both little girls. Luis talking about the familiar stranger, but didn't that, the fact that both of them had known him—and Marla and Alice not pals, not visiting each others' homes— rule out at one fell swoop any casual acquaintances of the parents', the insurance men and probably repair men and all such visiting the homes? You could say.

All right. What else?

Neighbors, thought Hackett. Neighbors? These days, in the big city, who really knew much about neighbors? Neighbor-hoods were different in different places, sure. Some places—he was going by what Angel said—people in and out of each other's houses, the morning coffee, borrowing sugar, and so on. And others, people friendly but not in and out. What about those blocks down there, around that school? Neigh-bors—

Hackett got up and went into Mendoza's office for the Los Angeles County guide. He looked at the detailed map of that area with interest.

The Foster house on Morton. The Pickens apartment on Laguna. The Stark house on Lucretia. Yes, but the Larsens lived on Delta, and Alice had often gone there to play with Trudy. Coming home, she'd have maybe passed down a couple of streets that she'd have used on the way to school too, and Marla went to the Fosters' after school, walking down some of those same streets.

"By God, I wonder," said Hackett to himself. It was a thing to think about. It was indeed.

Along those streets, people. And really, who would know much about them, unless they'd lived there a long time? Quite a few apartments along there. And very possibly there had been, along those streets, at least a few people—a few men— familiar in a sense to the little girls. Both little girls separately.

Old Mr. Jones out weeding his flower bed.

Young Mr. Smith working on his sports car.

Maybe saying Hi, and How's school?—otherwise friendly.

So when, say, Marla on her way back to school that morn- ing was hailed by young Mr. Smith and offered a ride, it prob- ably wouldn't cross her mind to think of him as the stranger she'd been warned about.

Only, really, how to start any hunt among the neighbors? For blocks around? Well, take just these blocks which both little girls would have walked on—Just for fun, take a look at who lived there. And hope, maybe, for the hunch.

It was an idea, anyway.

"Yes, that's it," said Mrs. Ruggles. "Funny-looking dog."

"We thought it was," said Alison. Cedric sat down beside her on the porch of this unpretentious California bungalow. He had not offered Mrs. Ruggles the polite paw. His attitude now was a patient waiting for the interview to be over. He had turned out to be well trained to a leash.

Mrs. Ruggles was about thirty-five, thin, and sandy-haired, and she had on a pair of bright turquoise-blue stretch pants and a pink shell top. "Chester was always daft about animals," she said. "Just daft. He told me he paid a hundred dollars for it when it was just a pup. Can you beat it?"

"We thought," said Alison, feeling exactly like a Benedict Arnold, "that he must have been thrown clear when the ac- cident happened, and then somehow found his way down off the freeway into Hollywood. He got into my car on a side street down from Yucca. And I put advertisements in—"

"Oh, I never thought to look at the ads," said Mrs. Ruggles. She hadn't asked Alison in. "Did you?"

"Yes, the *Citizen,* and the *Times* too. And I had our doctor —the vet, I mean—look at him, and he's fine. But when my husband found out—you see, he's a—"

"Well, that's good," said Mrs. Ruggles. "The only reason I

bothered, it must be worth something. I mean, if Chester paid a hundred bucks—"

"Yes," said Alison. She had never taken such a violent dislike to anyone at first sight as Mrs. Ruggles. The woman was absolutely obnoxious, she thought. *Desagradable, absolutamente.*

"They had a lot of cats too. Back where they lived. But they put all those in a place boards them, when they came out to visit."

Alison said, "Oh." She hoped very much that all the cats would find nice new homes; but obviously she couldn't do anything about that. "Well—I suppose he belongs to you. Or your husband." Was she the sister or sister-in-law? Luis hadn't said. "I just thought—my husband said—" But, Luis, I feel like a traitor. He's such a darling, and this—

"Cost a fortune to feed," said Mrs. Ruggles. "Lord, *I* don't want it. Nor Bill. But it must be valuable. And I suppose it does belong to us, sure. It was just terrible, poor Chester and Mary Jo and both the kids, an awful tragedy."

And a hypocrite too, thought Alison—just saying it like that, not even pretending much—really a most obnoxious woman, and the husband didn't sound much nicer. It was a very peculiar thing that whatever very nice people must have had Cedric up to now should possess such relatives.

"Yes, it was," she said. "Terrible. Er—what will you do with him?"

Mrs. Ruggles looked at Cedric indifferently. "Chester said he had papers on it. What they call a pedigree, you know. I'd better write and get those, I guess. If he paid a hundred bucks for it when it was just a pup, somebody maybe'll buy it, if I advertise. If nobody does, the pound 'd take it, but I'll see if I can get something for it first. Anyway, it is ours and I'll take it off your hands, Mrs.—what'd you say?—I wouldn't have bothered, mention it to the cops, but Chester said—"

Really, the most horrible woman Alison had ever met in her life. Cedric got up, rattling his collar, and put a paw on her ankle. Wasn't it time, he seemed to ask, that they left this place?

Alison felt it was long past time. There was, of course, Luis. *De veras.* But she had been married to Luis Rodolfo Vicente Mendoza long enough to know this and that about him.

"Mrs. Ruggles," she said, "if I gave you a hundred dollars for him, would that be all right? As long as you intend to sell him—"

The woman looked astonished. *"You* want it? A hundred dollars?" Her eyes looked calculating: she looked at Alison's alligator pumps and the new forest-green suit with interest. At least, Alison reflected, she wasn't wearing the emerald earrings. "Well, Chester paid a hundred when it was just a pup—if you want it—I mean, it's grown up and all now—"

"I'll give you two hundred," said Alison briskly. "I think that's fair. I'll write a check right now—"

"Well, that's certainly O.K. with me, if you want it. You understand, it being worth something, otherwise I wouldn't have bothered the cops—"

Ten minutes later Alison led Cedric back to the Facel-Vega. "And I don't care what he says," she said to Cedric, starting the engine. "I'd have been no less than a murderer to leave you there. That woman! *Por Dios,* that woman!"

Mendoza got back to the office at eleven-thirty: there had been the usual delay in court, but once they got to the inquest it was short and sweet. The expectable open verdict.

Hackett passed along his newest idea, Higgins drifting in in time to hear that. Mendoza said, *"Es posible.* It is an idea. Having nowhere else to look, we'll try it. Did anything else show on the new job?"

"Not unless the lab turns up something." Hackett was still trying to get that report finished; he turned back to the typewriter.

Ten minutes later Scarne came in and said, "Fortunately for us, most of them are fools."

"Meaning what?" Higgins looked up from his report on the suicide.

"Meaning that your latest boy left his prints all over that register and the front door. At least it looks suggestive," said

Scarne. "Lovely prints. I ran the ones from the register through first, and he showed right away. One John Edward Milner, in our records. Then we got to matching them and he'd left some on the door too."

"Oh, you don't say," said Hackett. "What's his pedigree?"

"You can look, I just established that he is in our records."

"Prints," said Higgins. "A guy with a record. You would think the merest ounce of common sense—"

"Which is just what most of them haven't got," said Hackett. "Which we learn all over again nearly every day, don't we? You go pull that pedigree."

"You go. I've got this damn report to type. Some time today," said Higgins, "I've got to pick up Laurie's birthday present. I had it engraved with her initials, they said it'd be ready yesterday. And I suppose Mary'll give me hell, but damn it, Art, they're good kids and they don't get many treats and she wants a wristwatch so—" He looked uneasy and defiant.

Hackett went down to records and pulled the pedigree of John Edward Milner. He had quite a long one. All the way from the petty juvenile things to two counts of armed robbery, one of burglary. He had been convicted in 1961 on that last count, a five-to-ten sentence, which said he probably hadn't been out long. The last address given was on Fourteenth Street. A long time back, it was very unlikely he was living there now, but even in a big city people sometimes stayed put. It was a first place to look, anyway.

After lunch.

"The more I think about your little idea, Arturo," said Mendoza over lunch, "the better I like it. The neighbors. The two little girls meandering down the residential streets, maybe stopping to talk to the friendly neighbors. Neighbors in a wide sense—two, four, six blocks from home. And ninety-nine times out of a hundred, those people are just ordinary people, but it just could be—on one of those blocks down there—one of them isn't. Old Mr. Jones, young Mr. Smith. And also, just possibly, somebody new to us. I did have the hunch, he's not in Records, we won't find him that way. Not our records."

"Which is also a factor," said Higgins somewhat sleepily. "People do move. Old Mr. Jones known as a menace to minors back in Philly—not known to us here."

"I think," said Mendoza, "after somebody checks out this Milner—it's about a thousand to one he's still at that address, but we'd better find out who his pals are around here, and put the word around we want him—we'll do a little looking there, anyway. I want that one like hell. As to how—" He finished his sandwich and poured himself more coffee. "Just on a first cast, let's ask the parents first. If either Marla or Alice knew any of the immediate neighbors—or ones farther away—ever mentioned talking to, mmh, old Mr. Jones or young Mr. Smith. I don't suppose we'll get much from the unimaginative Mrs. Pickens—" he grinned at Grace across the table. "You can tackle her, Jase. Our sweet-talker. But you never know, something may emerge. Just a little something, to give us another lead."

"I don't know what the man will say, *achara*," said Mrs. MacTaggart.

"Well, let him rave," said Alison. "Just let him. *I* live here too—and they're my offspring as well as his—if I choose to buy them a present, it's also my money. And these blessed cats like him too—and after *all*, Máiri—"

The offspring were earsplittingly voluble with joy, and she had to raise her voice.

"I just cannot think what he'll say," said Mrs. MacTaggart fearfully. "Though I will agree you juist couldna have done anything else. Her saying the pound."

"Of course not. And I'll argue him around," said Alison confidently. "You wait and see."

Before he went to see Mrs. Pickens, Jason Grace attended Alice Stark's funeral. Of duty. He didn't think much of the idea that a killer tended to show up at a victim's funeral, but occasionally they did; and just a while ago, in fact, one had, to break an otherwise baffling case. So he went.

The funeral, surprisingly, was up at Forest Lawn. Maybe a

rather expensive funeral. Reporters there, quite a few people: the reporters bothering them now, with two little girls killed. And nothing to give the reporters.

But he did spot one little thing which faintly surprised him. One of the mourners. He hadn't met that one: Mendoza and, he thought, Hackett had been the ones to interview that one. But that had been on the first little girl.

He thought it was a thing to mention to the Lieutenant.

After he'd seen Mrs. Pickens.

Chapter Fourteen

HIGGINS snatched half an hour after lunch to pick up Laura's birthday watch, and drop in on Landers with some more paperback books. Landers was still grumbling about getting stuck there, damn-fool berserk citizen just by a fluke shot putting him here, for God's sake. "If they'd let me go home—"

"What? You're waited on hand-and-foot here, and a couple of those nurses I passed are good-lookers."

"If you want to know," said Landers, "that's the reason I want to go home. That afternoon nurse—I'm scared to death of her. I've got the awful feeling she's got designs on me, George."

Higgins grinned. "Don't be so egotistical. Most nurses have got a lot of common sense, and what sensible female would want to take up with a cop these days?"

Landers brightened a little. "There's something in that."

Grace didn't get anything at all useful out of Margaret Pickens. She stared and asked, "What do you mean? People on the street? I always warned her careful not to talk to strangers—"

"Not people she'd think of as strangers, Mrs. Pickens," said Grace patiently. "People like—oh, the man out watering his lawn, or washing his car, who maybe said hello to her. Or the mailman. Or—"

"I don't hardly get any mail. I don't think Marla ever saw the mailman, he comes about noon—"

"But people like that. Do you see what I mean?"

She shook her head. She looked completely defeated by life, incapable of making an effort even of imagination; perhaps least of all that. "I always warned her," she repeated drearily. "Marla was a good girl. I don't know how—"

After a while Grace gave it up. It was too much to expect of her. All he had got was that they had lived in that apartment for five years, since before the husband had left her. So Marla would have known the neighborhood very well, and quite possibly had known a few of the people in it for all the time her memory ran back. But, an eight-year-old these days, in the city, covered a good-sized area—going to school, running errands for Mother—maybe eight, ten, twelve square blocks.

How was a bedeviled team of Homicide men, with other things coming up, going to cover an area that size and look at everybody inside it?

He did have the rather definite feeling that the Lieutenant ought to hear about his observation at Alice's funeral. He went back to the office and found it empty save for Sergeant Lake. "He wants the word put out about this Milner," said Lake. "Glasser's wandering around all the low bars spreading it. I suppose you can go and help."

"You think of the nicest ideas," said Grace. "I just can't think of a place I'd rather be on a dark depressing February afternoon"—it was threatening to rain again—"than a series of low bars on the Row."

"Well, nobody twisted your arm to make you take the oath," said Lake reasonably, and Grace laughed.

"How right you are. O.K., I'll do about an hour of it and come back—I want to see the boss."

Mendoza had, for no very valid reason, brought along the white cardigan. He held it in its brown-paper wrapping on his lap while they started to talk with the Starks. The little bungalow on Lucretia was very neat and trim, in and out: Stark evidently a gardener on his days off. The living room might be stereotyped—early American, and rather too faithfully like the illustrations in any home magazine—but it was very tidy and immaculate and comfortable.

The Starks looked dumbly at the men from Homicide, the dapper mustached Mendoza and big sandy Hackett, there in their quiet, ordinary-citizen room where death had brought them, unexpected and unfamiliar.

"I don't know what to say," said Mrs. Stark. "I don't—I don't remember Alice ever mentioning—anyone like that. Any one—of the neighbors, or—oh, she knew the Fieldings next door, they're both in their eighties and fond of children, but —I can't think of anyone else—right around here."

Mendoza gave her time to assimilate the idea. He unfolded the sweater from its wrappings and handed it to her.

"It's—Where did you find it? It's Alice's, the one she—"

"Yes. But it wasn't as dirty as that when she started to school on Friday, was it?"

"No, it certainly wasn't—" she fingered it tenderly and yet with a fastidious repugnance—the killer would have handled it. "It was—I'd washed it the day before." She looked at him, and her mouth quivered. "Wh-whatever help we can give you, we've got to try—but there's nothing more to tell you—I'm sorry—" and she put her head down on the cardigan and wept.

"Ah, Marian," said her husband. "Please, it's no good, honey—"

"Mr. Stark," said Hackett quietly, "if you'll try to think back —was Alice ever with you when you, maybe, stopped at a service station, your regular one, for gas, or—? How many of the people along this block, the next block, did she know by sight? By name? People who might have talked to her?"

Stark just shook his head. His face looked ravaged. "I don't know. I don't know. I'm sorry. The minister saying, God's will. She was only eight. Only—And the only one we ever had. I don't know, maybe it was foolish—but I wanted a nice service —a real nice service for my little girl. A pretty place for her to be, like up there in Forest Lawn. She—she went to Sunday school, you know. She—What? The neighbors? Well, they've been nice. The Fieldings sent over a cake—"

Mendoza felt frustrated. How the hell to go on hunting this

one, on this nebulous little idea? What in hell's name that
lead could mean—furniture glue and turpentine, for God's—

"—Mrs. Gebhardt brought over a casserole and cried just as
if Alice'd been her own—"

Marian Stark looked up slowly from the dirty white
sweater. "Everybody's been good," she said brokenly, "and it's
not as if we've lived here long either. Only two years, since we
had enough for the down payment. A time like this, you find
out how people really are. You said—people she knew? But
she didn't know many people, really—eight years old. In school,
the teachers—and we haven't many close friends, we don't
entertain a lot. And we told you she was shy. Awfully timid.
She hadn't many friends her own age, even. My—little—Alice."
She sobbed once. "We thought she'd grow out of it. It wasn't
until she was four or five we could leave her with a baby-sitter
at all, and she hated it, so we didn't much. And it's not so easy
to find a woman you feel you can trust, who's kind and reliable
—we were lucky to find one like that here, and Alice did like
her. Took to her right away. But even with Mrs. Foster, she
didn't like us to leave her too long—"

"*Mrs. Foster?*" said Mendoza.

"Why, yes. Mrs. Foster—she doesn't live far away, and Alice
never minded going there for just a few hours in the early
evening—we never left her late—"

Mendoza said to himself, "*Esto me da en que pensar.* But
what am I thinking about?"

"Coincidence," said Hackett. "What does it say?"

Mendoza got up slowly, and there was a little cold glint in
his eye that Hackett had seen before. "The familiar stranger,"
he said, and gave a little gasp. "*Por Dios.* We've been talking
about him for days. And all of us blind as the proverbial bats
—it never crossed our minds any more than it crossed Marla's
or Alice's—but the hell of a lot less excuse for us than them—"

"What are you talking about?" Hackett got up too.

"The one man we know they both knew—must have known.
The man we never thought about. Because he was—back-
ground. Come on," said Mendoza. "Let's go find out."

The house was the same, gloriously untidy and shabby but imbued with the sense of welcome and comfort the woman somehow imparted to it. The kind, shallow, rather stupid woman. She was dressed in black again, and had come to the door carrying a pair of cheap black high-heeled pumps. "Oh, you got to excuse me, I just got home and my feet were hurting, I was just—Come in. You want to see me again about something? I just been to Alice's funeral. I had to go on the bus, Frank was working—"

They came into the muddled, cluttered living room. "By the way, Mrs. Foster," said Mendoza, "I don't think we've ever heard where your husband works?"

She looked surprised. "Frank? Why, he's got a job with this big string of secondhand stores—a Mr. Owens owns it—all over L.A. County. He makes deliveries and pickups and does odd jobs round the warehouse, you know. Why? What was it you wanted—?"

"You take care of quite a few children here, one way and another," said Mendoza. "Don't you? Baby-sitting?"

"I like kids. Sure. We never had any of our own. And I had to have that operation—"

"Sometimes parents leave the kids here, and sometimes you go to the homes?"

"Sure. Why?"

"Do you drive, Mrs. Foster?"

"No, I don't. Frank'll take me if I'm going to somebody's house, and pick me up."

"And when the kids are here, sometimes, in the evenings, so is he. Isn't he?"

Suddenly she looked frightened. "Well, acourse—"

"Yes. Haven't any of the little girls you've had here ever complained to you, maybe, that Mr. Foster was saying or doing funny things? That he—?"

She began to back away from him slowly, her rose color draining away. She brought up against the couch covered with a miscellany of objects, and collapsed onto a heap of old movie magazines.

"You—you aren't tellin' me *that was Frank?*" she said

hoarsely. "That—*killed*—Oh, Lord, oh, no, it couldn't be—it just couldn't be. He's all over that foolishness now. I know he is. That doctor he got sent to back in Chicago, he cured him of —wanting to do like that. He said—"

Mendoza seemed to swell as he bent toward her; his face went white with fury. "*Mujer estúpida*—you damned stupid fool of a—are you telling us, are you *telling* us he's done it *before* —and you deliberately brought children into this house and let him—" The incredulous anger silenced him; he stared at her in astonishment and contempt.

"My God," said Hackett under his breath. "She couldn't be —*nobody* could be as—"

She shrank away from him and began to cry in little gasps. "Oh, no, it couldn't be—he's cured of all that—it wasn't anything much, anyways—oh, oh—back when we lived in Chicago, and I—kept the kids sometimes, working mothers, some of the little girls said he—and the police come, and he—oh, oh—there was a trial, and they said—about the doctor, and treatment—"

"The head doctor," said Hackett. "My God, Luis, but after *that,* she—"

"Oh, oh, oh," she moaned. "It just couldn't be Frank. I just couldn't believe—"

And they couldn't believe. In such utter stupidity.

They found him fitting a broken leg back onto an old straight chair, in the workshop of the big warehouse on Seventy-seventh Street. On the way in, they had passed a white Ford pickup truck parked in the lot. And they had had a word with Owens Junior, a sturdy red-faced young man in charge of the warehouse.

"Impound?" he said. "Police? The Ford? What're you trying to pull, some kind of gag? What *is* this? Foster? A very reliable —My God," as he looked at the badges, "you *are* police. What *is* this?"

"We'll be towing the Ford in for laboratory examination, Mr. Owens. So just keep away from it, and tell your other men to do the same. Where's Foster?"

"Out back. I guess. The workshop. What's he done, for—?" Owens' voice died away at their expressions.

But Foster's expression didn't change at all when they stood over him and Mendoza told him they were taking him in to answer some questions about Marla and Alice. He crouched there over the old chair, a husky dark man in the mid-thirties, his dark eyes sunken deep in their sockets so that he looked, not furtive exactly, but secretive. He glanced up at them once, a quick flash, and dropped his eyes, and then he stood up slowly and picked up a piece of ragged cloth and began to wipe his hands. There was a bottle on the bench nearby, a sticky label half illegible on it: furniture glue. The odd jobs: perhaps refinishing furniture, painting, using the turpentine. Working in different stores owned by Owens Senior, so the glue and turpentine in the pickup.

"Did you understand me, Foster? We're—"

He nodded once.

So very carefully Mendoza warned him. He had the right to a lawyer, to remain silent. He nodded again. He walked out between them and got stiffly into the passenger seat of the Ferrari.

In an interrogation room downtown, he was no more talkative. Once in a while he answered a question; mostly he sat, head down, eyes blank, as if unhearing.

"Is he nuts, or building a defense that way?" asked Hackett in an interval.

"I don't think either one," said Mendoza. "I don't like him. Any way I don't like him, but if he acts like this in front of a jury they'll never convict—he looks too much like the honest-to-God lunatic."

Grace came in and heard about it, and said he would be eternally damned. "Do you mean to say that fool woman *knew* he had tendencies that way and didn't think twice about fetching in the innocent little girls under the same roof? You would think anybody would know better—"

"A very stupid woman, Jase," said Mendoza. "But yes, you would."

They went back and tackled him again, and he went on

staying dumb. The only thing he'd admitted was knowing Marla and Alice. He was still sitting there looking blank and almost half-witted when Piggott came in and they broke off again.

"Jimmy told me. I don't believe it," said Piggott. "I do not. I don't mean *him*, but about that woman. She *knew* he was like that, and—"

"I know, I know," said Mendoza. *"¡Vaya por Dios!* But—"

"A little lower than the angels," said Hackett. *"Is* he insane? The way he's acting? Really not responsible?"

And Piggott, that mild-mannered man, said quite sharply for Piggott, "Not responsible? That's a phrase I don't like to hear bandied about, if you don't mind. Not responsible? We're all responsible for whatever we do or don't do, for the Lord's sweet sake. Most people, whether they're technically insane or not, know what they're doing while they're doing it. I'll tell you what it was with him, it was the devil, that's all. Going up and down converting whom he can."

And Foster heard that, and said suddenly, loudly, "That's right. That's got to be right. I was late for work that morning, I'd just backed out to the street when Marla came out of the house—I never see her go in, the side door. And it musta been the devil in my heart—make me follow her down to the corner, say, I'll drive you back. She never thought about it. I knew she wouldn't. I knew. All the times she was at the house—pretty little kid—I wanted—but I was scared. Everybody'd know—after. But right then, I knew nobody'd know she'd been with me. Nobody to see her there. And it was easy—she was chattering along, never noticed where we were till we started up the hill, and I said, little ride in the park—she never knew nothing was wrong till I stopped and made her get out. And I—She'd have told. I knew that."

They were around him then. "And Alice?" said Mendoza. But he didn't seem to hear Mendoza; his deep-sunk eyes blinked up at Piggott's thin dark face.

"The devil," he muttered. "The devil getting inside me— don't know why I wanted—so awful bad—to do that. The little girls. Like I had to—had to—Stronger than me, but all the time I knew it was wrong. Alice. Scared of a lot o' things, little

Alice—but not of me. At first. She knew me, Rhoda's husband. Played games with me—at the house. She didn't know the devil had got inside me. I hadn't thought, with Marla. She was just there—it just happened. But I thought about it, with Alice. All that week. Oh, yes. I knew she went home for lunch, and I knew which gate she'd come out. I had a pickup to make, clear over to Montebello, nobody'd notice how long I was gone —traffic like it is. I—" He looked at Piggott. "People say the devil he ain't real no more."

"He's real," said Piggott softly, "only no horns and tail to know him by. Inside men's hearts, Foster."

"Yes, that's right," said Foster. "That's right. Only—only it was me let him in. It was just me."

"You remember that, Foster," said Piggott. "Nobody else unlocked the door for him."

They booked him into the Alameda jail and applied for the warrant. Lake called Palliser to tell him, and Palliser said, "I don't believe it. That anybody could be so stupid—"

"Well, that's the kind we're dealing with mostly, isn't it?" said Lake wearily.

They were to find the physical evidence in the Ford pickup: the glue, the turpentine. They were to find that Foster's blood type was A–B, to match the scrap of cloth missing from a pair of his tan pants where Marla had bitten him. And his old gray Chevy sedan. But they had his confession, to be repeated before a lawyer later, and they hoped it would hold tight at his trial. Which remained to be seen: their job was just to catch them, collect the evidence.

Hackett went home and told Angel about it while Sheila clambered all over him and Mark demanded praise for the day's crayon production. "Honestly, Art! You mean she knew he was —and deliberately—?"

"A little lower than the angels," said Hackett through a yawn. "We do run into them, my Angel. At least he's caught. We can hope they'll stash him away permanently."

Higgins went home and told Mary about it. "You mean the woman knew, and—? I can't believe it. Though talking about stupidity—and a primer example of pure stupidity I never heard than *that*—but at least he's caught, and let's hope some judge with common sense remaining puts him away for life —Speaking," said Mary, "of stupidity—that wristwatch. You—"

"Look," said Higgins, "they don't get many extra-special treats, Mary. Once in a while—"

"I do not believe," said Mary, "in indulging children. Whatever they want they get. It's not very realistic training for real life."

"Well, no," said Higgins. "I agree with you. But once in a while, Mary—and she wanted it so much—"

Mary bit her lip, and her gray eyes smiled at him. "You still trying to make it up to Bert's good kids? Like that, George?"

"Well, for God's sake," said Higgins, startled, "no. For God's sake! If you want to know, damn it, she looks at me— that daughter of yours—with your funny gray eyes, and she can have anything I've got in spades. Which I guess goes without saying goes for you too. I never had a family to spoil, Mary. It's kind of fun."

Her smile quivered a little. "Well, just don't go overboard," she said, trying to sound severe.

Alison met Mendoza at the back door as he came in. He kissed her and said they'd got him, told her about Foster as they went into the kitchen. Mrs. MacTaggart, busy over the stove, listened interestedly.

"But, Luis! That woman—it's worse than stupid, when she knew—"

Mrs. MacTaggart said seriously, "A proverb I mind my grandda saying. A fool will throw stones down a well, a hundred men canna pull out. It is the fools make most of the mischief in the world, indeed."

"You needn't tell any cop, Máiri," said Mendoza. He poured himself an ounce of rye—for once El Señor wasn't around to demand his share—and went down the hall to the living room, shedding his hat, jacket, and tie in the bedroom on the way.

Alison trailed after him anxiously. On the threshold of the living room he stopped short.

"*¡Qu édemonio—!* What the devil—?"

In the middle of the room Cedric, large and hairy, was sprawled blissfully with Bast cuddled between his forepaws, her feet folded under her, purring, and Sheba making rhythmic bread against his shaggy side. He smiled widely at Mendoza.

"*Darling*," said Alison, "I just couldn't have left him with that awful woman—she said the *pound*. I couldn't. I felt like Benedict Arnold, honestly, to think of it. You wouldn't have wanted me to, if you'd *seen* her. She was only interested in the money. Thinking he was valuable, because he had papers— you know. She's going to send us the papers, incidentally. When she gets them. I'd have been a murderer. And the twins adore him, Luis, and he's so good with them—and—"

"*¡Ca!*" said Mendoza. "This idiotic clown of a shaggy dog—"

"Luis," said Alison dangerously. "I know you, maybe better than you think. You—"

Mendoza swallowed half the rye. "I did wonder if you would think about my cats at all. About Bast. She's taken quite a notion to the creature. And Sheba. Strange as it may seem. If anybody had told me—" Cedric shook the cats off, got up, and offered him a welcoming paw. He shook it gravely. "*Saludos, bufón.* And whatever my cats want, within reason, they get. Even if it is a clown of a shaggy dog."

"*Sí, querido,*" said Alison demurely. "I—mmh—rather thought so. I bought the large-sized dog bed for him. And a new leash. And a license."

"So you thought of that. *Bueno.*" Cedric lay down again and Sheba began to chew his left ear. "We are, after all, supposed to be on the side of the law."